SONG OF THE MAGDALENE

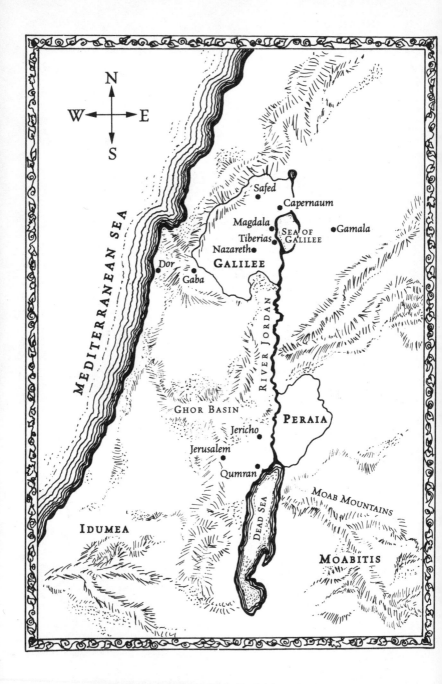

SONG OF
THE MAGDALENE

DONNA JO NAPOLI

SCHOLASTIC PRESS ❖ NEW YORK

Published by Scholastic Press, a division of Scholastic Inc.,
Publishers since 1920.
555 Broadway, New York, New York 10012

Library of Congress Cataloging-in-Publication Data

Napoli, Donna Jo. 1948-
Song of the Magdalene by Donna Jo Napoli.
p. cm.
Summary: Tells the story of Miriam, a young girl being raised by her
widowed father in ancient Israel, who grows up to be Mary Magdalene.
ISBN 0-590-93705-7
1. Mary Magdalene, Saint—Juvenile fiction. [1. Mary Magdalene,
Saint—Fiction. 2. Saints—Fiction.] I. Title.]
PZ7.N15Sr 1996
[Fic]—dc20 96-7066
CIP AC

12 11 10 9 8 7 6 5 4 3 2 1 6 7 8 9/9 0 1/0

Printed in the U.S.A. 37
First printing, October, 1996

❖

FOR MY SISTER MARIE, WITH LOVE

ACKNOWLEDGMENTS

I thank Dorcas Allen, Shannon Allen, Rebecca Alpert, Leila Berner, David Bookspan, Brenda Bowen, Wendy Cholbi, Janet Sternfeld Davis, Stuart Davis, Nathaniel Deutsch, Amy Eerdmans, Marla Feldman, Barry Furrow, Elena Furrow, Thad Guyer, Lindgren Lammers, Joanna Lehmann, A.-J. Levine, David McKay, Barry Miller, Lucia Monfried, Brenda Nixon, Shelley Nixon, Joel Perwin, Miriam Peskowitz, Ramneek Pooni, Emmie Quotah, Emily Rando, Bill Reynolds, Jennifer Rosenblum, Ellen Ross, Sandy Sborofsky, Bob Schachner, Judith Schachner, Hadass Sheffer, David Sobel, Martin Srajek, Sarah Stockwell, Chuck Tilly, and Patricia Whitman, as well as Ms. Purnell's first period English class at Strath Haven High School in 1995–96. All of them did their best to keep me from errors of physiology, history, culture, religion, geography, and heart, and none of them is to be held responsible for the errors that remain.

I also thank my mother, Helen Napoli, who encouraged me to complete this story, and Linda Alter, whose Leeway Foundation gave me a grant at exactly the right moment to allow me to act on that encouragement.

Palestine of the first century is a place and time over which scholars disagree vehemently. Inevitably, I found myself often having to make choices over controversial issues. In those instances I let the story be my guide. For this is fiction and my goal is simply to tell the story.

SONG OF THE MAGDALENE

CHAPTER ONE

The first fit came out of the blue, out of the blue, blue sky.

Hannah was on our flat roof, hanging out the wash. I rejoiced in its colors, just as my mother used to. When I had my own house, I'd fill it with color. I'd even have purple. Hannah allowed no purple. Purple was the sign of power and Hannah was quick to quote her brother Daniel, the scholar, who eschewed marks of vanity. Daniel used to live nearby, before he went away to Alexandria. He came daily to teach Hannah's son Abraham. He had much to say on vanity. I didn't care to hear about vanity. I secretly longed for a wide cloth belt, highly decorated with purple embroidery. In the shape of animals. Maybe birds. Birds with gaudy plumage, flying free. "I'm going, Hannah," I said, breathless at the thought of flying free myself.

Hannah looked at me quickly. "Where?"

Though Hannah was but a servant, I owed her an account of my whereabouts. "The valley." I looked down now at my feet that wanted to dance in the grasses. Dance and dance till I dropped from exhaustion. If I hadn't loved Hannah, I would have left without hesitation. "Hannah, I have to."

Hannah clicked her tongue in sympathy. She picked up the laundry basket and looked at me. "Miriam, there are chores still."

"I've worked side by side with you since dawn. The morning is almost gone." My voice came high with urgency. If I didn't go, I'd burst from within. The open beckoned me.

"The morning is barely begun." Hannah's tone stayed flat, but her face held no hope that I would listen. She sighed. "Be alert."

I knew she spoke from fear. I did not truly believe in the danger that tightened Hannah's face. The danger was from the tongues of the villagers. If they told Father I was out alone, if he learned that Hannah kept my new wanderings secret from him, he might forget his charity toward her. He might send Hannah away. Then who would provide for her and her crippled son Abraham? I knew this was Hannah's fear. I could not believe it of Father. Still, I would use extreme caution. I would let no one guess. I felt like a liar.

I stopped at Mother's grave and kissed the earth. Then I took the only road eastward, the road that passed by the well. The valley lay just beyond.

The well was busy that morning, like every morning. I warmed to the cadences of the women's voices as they filled their long-necked jars. The children played noisily, straying into the tall grasses. On the large rocks off toward the village two young men sat. I knew they discussed Deborah. Deborah was twelve, and those two years between her and me set us a world apart — for Deborah was ready for betrothal. Today I could see her name suited her — "Deborah" meant "honey bee" and today she was the queen of bees.

I thought of the saying of our people: You should be like your name. What did "Miriam" mean? How did I get my name? I was not a bitter blow to my parents, so they surely had not built my name around the word *mrr*. No, I was wished for: *maram*. I was loved, like the Egyptian word *mry*. Would I ever be fat — *mr*? I laughed. Someday I'd be fat with child. Fat like Mother was in the last months of her life. Maybe my name foretold the future. Maybe I'd have child after child after child.

I looked at the women as I walked by. They talked continuously and rapidly. I could make out snatches.

"When Simon the tax collector comes knocking, we will fill his ears, not his moneybags."

"As will we. He's collected more than enough coins already this year. Angry words are his due."

"Herod Antipas builds a city of disgrace. No proper Jew will live there."

"So our money, our work, it all goes for the Romans who will become the new Tiberians."

The loudest voices belonged to Naomi, wife of the fisherman Ezekiel, and Shiphrah, wife of the carpenter Jacob. I watched their arms wave, the sun glinting off gold bracelets. Neither woman knew poverty. Neither would suffer from the taxes the way most of the other women would. Yet they lamented as angrily as any. And they were deferred to, out of respect for their husbands.

I sat near a bush and leaned back on my elbows. There was no point in straining to hear. The story was the same, day after day. The whole of Galilee suffered under the collection of the taxes for building a new palace for Herod Antipas. The women of Magdala couldn't stop chattering about it.

Oh, I did know it wasn't simply chatter: Taxes were important. Still, on this lovely day, the talk of taxes seemed distant.

I looked across the women. Judith wasn't here yet. If Judith had been here, her eyes would have sought me. She'd have made a point of waving and watching over me. And before she left, she would have come close and murmured endearments I despised. I had often heard the women talking about her; I knew Judith wanted to marry Father. The knowledge made my insides quiver.

Father could take a wife, or even wives, if he

wanted. Few men had more than one wife, but Father was rich enough to afford more than one, and handsome enough to have his offer accepted. Yet, after Mother died, he lived with only me for a year. Then Hannah and her son Abraham moved in. Hannah had worked for us all my life, but her living with us was new and welcome, despite the villagers' whispers. People were curious about us . . . the odd family headed by a man who slept alone, the family that harbored a cripple, even though cripples were inhabited by demons.

But no one looked at me with curiosity now. Not even my best friend Sarah paid me any heed. Everyone was busy in another world — the women talking together, the children running about — a world I now exited from and observed as a stranger. For a moment I felt small. Like the baby in Salome's arms over there. Almost invisible.

I moved on my bottom behind the bush. Then I stood up and walked quickly. I stayed close to the bushes and barely breathed, though I loved the scent of the undergrowth — the myrtle and broom, the acanthus and wormwood. Now was not the time to indulge in their heady fragrances.

I knew shallow breaths moved one to the edge of life. If I could skim along the edge of life, perhaps I could slip away unnoticed. When I couldn't hear the children anymore, I took off my sandals, planted them by a lentisk bush, and ran.

I ran faster and faster, to the very heart of the wood. Only then did I finally stop and listen to the rush of the wind in the highest treetops, the rush of the blood in my veins.

When I emerged into a field, I lay on my back, my shift hiked up over my knees. Now the sun would work its warming magic. The sky was cloudless. No breezes. I wondered if the fishing boats to the east, on the Sea of Galilee, were as still as my heart.

On my back all I saw was the sky. The morning sky, without stars or moon, without clouds, has only one point of reference — the sun. But from where I lay, with the sun burning over the sea, the ball of fire was out of my line of vision. All was blue.

I sang a song to a tune I had made up. I didn't know any real tunes. Father sang often, but not at home. He sang in the house of prayer. Hannah told me about it, for I didn't go to the house of prayer. I didn't like the idea of being closed in, listening. I wanted to be outdoors, dancing. But Hannah went daily to pray for Abraham.

I didn't pray really — at least not in the sense that men did. The men said prayers three times a day at fixed hours. But the women were free from those commandments. We had other duties. I helped Hannah in keeping Sabbath. I helped in minding the dietary laws. I smiled at the requisite fourth toe, the hind toe, on the fowl we ate. I peeled the sac off the gizzard with care. I picked the scales off fish so painstakingly that never once did I tear the skin and thus ruin the flesh. I knew my most important job was to grow strong and be a good wife and mother someday. A good wife did everything she could to make it possible for her husband to obey Jewish Laws. A good mother did everything she could to teach her sons and daughters the Jewish Laws so they could grow up and be good husbands and wives and, in their turn, good parents.

Everything was aimed at ensuring that the past of Israel would live in the present and endure into the future. Israel was the people we were part of. Every Jew everywhere belonged to Israel. I belonged to Israel. My future husband belonged to Israel.

I had no idea whom I would marry. A girl from a family rich like mine would ordinarily have had a marriage arranged years ago. But Mother had turned a deaf ear to parents seeking matches for their sons. Mother believed in love between husband and wife. Father said one of the greatest pleasures of life was its unlikelihoods. Mother was an unlikelihood. She married Father for love.

I wanted to know more about this kind of love. But Hannah bent over her sewing with small noises of annoyance whenever I asked. And if I persisted, she coughed. Had Hannah loved the father of her son Abraham?

Mother made Father promise that I could choose my own husband when I came of age. She wanted love for me, as well. I was happy at the thought.

And now I sang that happiness in my own mixed-up version of a song about fawns. It was from one of our scrolls. I didn't read, of course. But I'd heard Abraham read it. We kept many scrolls because of him — because he needed something to do all day. And I'd spoken with Father about this fawn song, a song of mysterious love.

I sang loud and long. My breaths were as deep as the center of the sea. I was fully alive.

I expected everything good.

And out of the blue of the sky came a brightness that burst and dazzled. My eyes went dry like desert sand. My song caught in my throat. My mouth opened as if it wanted to swallow all of Israel. I couldn't close it. I tried, but everything, all of me, was stiff as stone. Stiff and wild. I knew nothing, understood nothing, but fear. That was the last thing I remembered, desperately trying to close my mouth, feeling the dry burn of exposure that will not end, sealed in the fear.

I must have slept. For when I knew again where I was, the sun was high overhead. My lips were hard and cracked. I opened my mouth and the tight crust of saliva on my chin and cheeks pulled at my skin. I was warm, like on the hottest days of summer. I was weary, as though I'd run for hours. I stood up and looked down at my shift, grass-stained but whole. I stared at the cloth as the realization came.

It was wrong that my clothing should be whole, it was terribly wrong, for I knew my soul had been rent. I had struggled on the ground, locked in a grip I could not break. Had I really had a fit? Oh, I had! I had. Tears streamed down my cheeks. I doubled over in sobs, yielding to the huge, merciful grief that drowned thought.

But reason gradually returned, inevitable and cruel. I took stock. I knew the source of such fits. Everyone knew. A demon had taken up residence in the shell of my body. Just as a demon lived in Abraham. But this was my own personal demon of fits. In me. Inside me.

I wiped away my tears and waited to see what would happen next. I waited many hours. The sun moved through the afternoon. My neck strained like a coreopsis turning to the light.

I looked down at my long toes. If I were to die in the valley now, I would die barefoot, like one of the common children. Would that matter?

As evening came, I walked back in a daze. My sandals awaited me safely at the lentisk bush. I went home looking no different from how I had always looked.

The sky was still blue.

CHAPTER TWO

As I lay on my bed mat before the next dawn, I touched my ears, my eyes, the tip of my tongue. I traced the creases of my hands. These things that had always told me about the world, did these things serve me still? Would the demon within lie to me about the world I walked through? Would this demon betray me with my own senses?

I was aware of each rise and fall of my chest. I felt the darkness of our home, springtime damp, like the darkness of a cave.

I thought of the caves at Qumran, far to the south, on the northwest shore of the Dead Sea. On the first anniversary of Mother's death Father had gone on a private pilgrimage. He went all the way to Qumran to see a community of Essenes who lived near dry, white caves. When he returned, he talked late into the night with the village men, telling what he had learned, saying how these Qumran people believed that self-denial led to purity.

That was it: I was impure. Why else would this moment have brought the image of those caves? I had invited the demon of the fit into me with the power of some inner impurity. I was in need of being purged. The thought transfixed me. The happy girl who danced through the house and up the steps to our roof, who wove herself a path in and out of the laundry line, the girl who chattered stories to Abraham on rainy days and who had been Mother's treasure, that girl was filthy.

I hugged myself tight and opened my eyes.

I could not go to Qumran. I was a woman. I would not travel anywhere alone.

I rose from my bed mat and stood in the dark, patted by the breaths of Father and Hannah and Abraham, all asleep. My stomach growled. I hadn't eaten since breakfast the day before. The thought of a spring fig, immense and dark, made me swallow hard. Those figs would be ready just days after Passover. Soon now.

An old fig tree stood near our house. Father

pruned it round so that it shaded our home all through the summer and fall. He said fig trees were good for meditation; their thick foliage gave calm. I went outside and sat beneath the tree. Not a wasp buzzed. I opened my mind to whatever would come. An answer would surely come. Before long Hannah called me in to help start the day's chores.

After that I no longer expected sudden revelation or damnation. It was as though a heavy cloak had been draped across my shoulders and even a soul as impatient as mine couldn't but recognize that every step had to be measured. Every thought came wrapped.

For months I went to the valley any time I could. I had decided that it was my deception in going to the valley alone that had invited the demon. That was my impurity. So the valley should have been the last place I'd go. But the valley was the only place I could go. It was the only place I could be sure no one would see me if a fit came again. And I had to make sure no one saw me in a fit. For if they did, I would join the outcasts of society.

Oh, Father would let me live with him still; I wouldn't wander the streets with the lame and those who babbled nonsense, my hand open for the alms that every Jew gave freely to the beggars. But the eyes of the villagers would look upon me with pity. Some might even carry a locust's egg or a fox's tooth in my presence — a charm to keep my demon from entering them. I refused to suffer such treatment. They would never see me in a fit.

My behavior showed a lack of faith, I knew. I should have gone directly to the mikvah and immersed myself completely in the ritual bath. After all, that's what women did after their monthly blood came. Hannah had told me about it. The blood would flow from me within a few years, making me unclean. While the blood flowed, I would be restricted in what and whom I touched. And soon after it stopped flowing, I would go to the mikvah and come home again pure. But it wasn't just women after their monthly blood who went to the mikvah — anyone who felt the need of cleansing could go. I had gone once myself, three years before — after Mother's funeral. If I went there now with my heart open, maybe the Creator would have mercy on me. Maybe the Creator would cleanse me of my demon.

But if I went to the mikvah, all would know I was unclean. They would wonder. They would ask. And if the Creator did not choose to cleanse me, I would have exposed myself for naught.

I thought of telling Father. I could ask him to take me to a healer. I was ready to drink the water of Dekarim, extracted from the roots of palm. I was ready to walk to the hot baths at El Hamma on the Sea of Galilee. I was willing, oh so willing. I would even go to an exorcist. Hannah had taken Abraham to an exorcist in Capernaum long ago.

I approached Father once. "Father, may I speak with you?"

Father smiled. "Yes, Miriam. Later."

I watched as he took off his shoes, washed his hands, and unfolded his tallith — the prayer shawl — carefully. Of course it was prayer time. I knew that. I just hadn't been thinking, I'd been so enveloped in my own need. I put out my fingertips and touched the feather tassel tips of the tallith. Mother wasn't clever at embroidery, so

Father's tallith had been bought. But Mother had added these tassels. They were white, like the original tassels. The only difference was that she had counted out the threads herself and knotted them. Each corner had a tassel of eight threads, totaling thirty-two — the number that matched the word for "heart." When Father prayed, knots of Mother's love brushed his arms.

I didn't wait for the end of his prayers. I couldn't bear witnessing my parents' love in that tallith — a love that seemed to swathe Father and distance me in my present isolation. I left.

I thought often of trying again to talk with Father. But every time the thoughts came, the knowledge followed: The Creator was the only true healer for a malady such as mine. After all, when Abraham went to the exorcist, no good had come of it. And last year when Shiphrah and Jacob brought their deformed baby girl to a traveling exorcist, the baby died in his hands.

So I didn't tell Father. And I hardly saw him, anyway. The long, hot season was always his busiest time for arranging trade. He stayed away for two or three weeks at a time.

When Father returned from a journey, he lingered around the house for a day or two, praying thanks to the Creator and renewing himself. On those days, I tended our kitchen garden. This could not be a sham. If Father was to find me at home, I would be home as a righteous woman devoted to the details of daily family life.

I grew lentils, beans, cucumbers, peppers, lettuce. I dug the earth with a vengeance new to me. The perimeter was onions and shallots and leeks. The area most in the sun was reserved for eggplant. The area most in the shade overflowed with chicory, endive, cress, and parsley. Everything thrived. The irony spurred me on. I reserved a section for a rock garden and the purslane spread there as though it were on the naked shores of the Dead Sea, the shores Father had described. Everything, everything thrived.

Hannah didn't mind it when I wouldn't go with her to the well, for the garden this year did much better than it had ever done under her care. No weed strayed into this dirt without being plucked mercilessly. No beetle nibbled on a lettuce leaf without being crushed by my thumbnail. If I kept vigilant, if I worked assiduously, a fit could not take me by surprise.

When Father was busy with trade, however, I went to the valley early in the morning and came home late at night. Hannah said it wasn't right that I should spend so many hours alone. She invited me to join her in making bread and spinning wool. She looked at me with eyes that longed to help me solve the secret problem she sensed growing within me. I tried to soothe her, but I failed. Hannah had lived with us too long not to recognize my wanderings as flight. But in one thing I succeeded: Hannah swore to keep my confidence. She told Father nothing of my visits to the valley.

Each silence on her part, each confidence on my part, while they didn't make us grow closer to one another, made us grow separate from Father. There were days when I feared the loyalty of Hannah — when I questioned for the first time the need for the separateness of women.

And the claws of my deception tore at my soul. I was mindful to watch Father and Hannah for signs of vulnerability. I didn't worry about Abraham. He already knew a devil. Father and Hannah, however, might need protection. And so when Father raised his hands and said firmly,

"*Shema yisra'el*," calling upon Israel to listen, when Hannah inspected the meat carefully to make sure it had been completely bled, I rejoiced inside. They followed the laws; they were pious. Neither of them would become the host of a devil. Neither would need refuge.

The valley was my refuge. I climbed the sycamores and in the very treetops I sang. I begged the Creator to look upon me. To do what I could not bear to have any human do — to pity me. I begged the Creator to forgive me for not going to the mikvah, for coming to the valley, for whatever impurities I hid from myself. When I climbed down, I did not dance. I had given up dancing. This was my own kind of atonement. The Creator knew how much my feet had rejoiced in dancing before. The Creator knew that I atoned.

I hung my shifts in the brightest sunlight and watched them fade. And I never mentioned pomegranates. No more crimson for me. Mother's colors faded away.

No more fits came. But I didn't know whether that was because the Creator had heard me and answered my song prayers, or because the demon within was waiting quietly. In the absence of fits, there was no way to know. I sang, day in day out, week in week out. I walked and walked and walked. Each night I slept the sleep of exhaustion.

CHAPTER THREE

This self-imposed exile in the valley might have gone on forever if it weren't for Abraham. One day as I was leaving the house, he called to me.

Hannah had gone to the well early, as usual. She drew the water and returned before the women with children gathered there. She would indulge in talk with the older women, but never with the young mothers. Most days Hannah took Abraham with her. She pushed him in a handcart Father had fashioned. It was because of Abraham that Hannah left when the women with children came to the well; I knew this. No mother ever had to tell her child not to go near Abraham, for Hannah whisked Abraham away before there was any need. No mother had to fear Abraham's demon.

I was allowed to stay behind at the well and

play if I liked. And in the old days, before my first fit, I had done that often. Now I never did. Now I usually didn't even accompany Hannah and Abraham to the well.

On this morning, however, Abraham was at home. The night before he had slept poorly. He woke cranky and complained of the heat. He said he couldn't bear the women's busy voices at the well that day. So Hannah left Abraham behind, propped outside the door, where he could catch a bit of air.

And he called to me.

At first I wasn't sure I had actually heard him. But he repeated, "Come here."

When I was small, I'd talked with Abraham many times, naturally, of nothing in particular. Other people found him hard to understand because his lips didn't move the right way. But I had no trouble knowing what he meant. Only these days we didn't have much to say to each other.

Still, I knew many things about Abraham. I knew he had little control over his legs and left arm. I knew his head stayed to one side because he couldn't right it. Had some flaw within Abraham's soul invited his demon, just as a flaw had invited mine?

I stood beside him and spoke gently. "What is it?"

He looked at me with steady eyes and I was afraid for a moment that he was unable to speak right then. I felt sure his eyes were telling me to pay attention.

My first thought was that he was in pain. He needed Hannah. "How are you?" I leaned close over him as I spoke.

"Afflicted."

I straightened up quickly.

Abraham showed his teeth. His shoulders moved. And I realized suddenly he was laughing. Abraham was making a joke of himself.

"You shouldn't talk that way."

"You shouldn't go off alone."

I suppressed a gasp and clasped my hands together. Of course Abraham would know I'd been off alone. We had no relatives hereabout, so there was no one's house that I could pass the day in. I should have expected Abraham would figure it out. He might have even overheard me tell Hannah I was going to the valley.

I pulled on my fingers, one after the other. "If you tell, it will be awful for everyone. Father will make Hannah go away."

"I won't tell."

Abraham was older than me. Above his lip a fine fuzz held bits of crumbs from his morning bread. He wouldn't tell. He knew what it would mean for his own life if he did. I folded my hands together and spoke with forced calm. "Why did you call me?"

"Take me with you."

"With me?" The words made no sense. "Where?"

"Wherever you go." Abraham moved his lips with care, working to make each word clear. "You're strong. Push me in the cart."

It was true. Though Abraham had to be at least thirteen, I was sure I weighed more than him, much more. Perhaps if he could stand, he'd be taller than me. But, then, Abraham had never stood. He never would. Abraham would never stand with the men in the holy services reciting prayers, though I knew he had memorized many of them. I had heard him mumbling holy words to himself as he sat before the fire on a winter's day. I had even heard him cry out passages from the scriptures in dreams sometimes. This youth who held the Talmud so dear would never make the traditional pilgrimages to Jerusalem with the other men, would never stand in the court of men in the Temple.

I considered his frail body now with dismay. "What would you do?"

"The same thing I do here."

I looked around. The late summer sun would grow too fierce for Hannah before long. She would return. If we were to go, we had to go fast. Could I push Abraham in the cart all the way to the valley? And how could the cart move among the tree roots? "I don't know. It would be hard."

"Lonely." Abraham spoke loudly. "Your feet used to fly around the room, graceful and light. Now you are anchored like a boat at midnight. You must be lonely. I am." His blue eyes sparkled. My own eyes were so dark, they bordered on black. But Abraham's eyes were like the Sea of Galilee. They were like the heavens. They compelled me.

I went to the side of the house and fetched the handcart, wondering whether I could really do it.

Hannah did it, and I was already almost as large as she. Still, I was only ten. I leaned over Abraham, hooked my arms under his armpits, and pulled him into the cart. He was even lighter than I'd thought. Hannah often lamented the fact that he barely ate, but now I was grateful for it.

His right hand managed to grasp the side of the cart. He struggled to get comfortable. I knew the position he preferred. I tucked his legs under him and rested him against the two logs Hannah kept in the cart for that purpose.

Abraham smiled. "Hurry."

A sudden thought stopped me. "Hannah will worry."

"Wonder."

I shook my head. "What are you saying?"

"Hannah will wonder, not worry. There is nothing to worry about for me. What more harm could come to me?"

I stared at Abraham. It was true that no one would harm him. Those who had palsy were ignored, not tormented. "You could have an accident. You could die."

"Is not death welcome?"

When Mother was dying, when she knew there was no chance left, she called me to her bed mat. She told me that the true calamity is not that we die, but that we must travel through life. I saved her words. No one before or since ever said such words to me. As I grew older, I came to see she had told me that to comfort me, so that I wouldn't fear for her as she passed from life. My mother died days after giving birth to Father's only son, who died as well. I remembered her voice, low and rich, full of whispers. I remembered her thick hair and long fingers. I slept under the gaze of her night eyes.

I respected Mother's last words. But now I reexamined them from my new position in life. I had been cast out from the holy, cut off from Israel and Israel's rewards. What did death promise me, the host of a demon?

Yet Abraham might be a sinner, too, and here he was, still believing that death was welcome. He must know fully the fate of sinners, for Abraham was knowledgeable. His uncle Daniel had taught him well, even though others behaved as though Abraham didn't exist. And Father had taken over Abraham's education after Daniel left. He taught him geography and history and so many things I'd never know. I looked at Abraham's intelligent eyes. Maybe Daniel and Father had been compelled by those eyes as much as I was now.

I folded Abraham's left arm across his chest and pushed the cart down the street. We turned off quickly at a path that led away from the well. It would be longer this way — much longer. But we couldn't risk being seen by Hannah or the watchful Judith or anyone else.

The cart went easily over the low grasses, but as they got higher, the going got more labored. Still, we were already out of sight of anyone going to or coming from the well. I slowed my pounding heart. I stooped and took off my sandals, slipping them into a corner of the cart. I would go before the Creator on feet that knew His earth. I pushed steadily, keeping my mind on the job at hand.

Abraham made small noises of appreciation, and before long I found myself looking around as though through his eyes, seeing the valley as though for the first time. The undergrowth was still free of roots, for the land didn't turn instantly to forest. Instead, it seduced with almost a casualness, beginning with the sparse olive groves, ashy gray and blue. These were the main source of our wealth. The fruits were pressed for oil that served in cooking, lighting, medicine, even in anointings in holy services. Next we passed the fruit orchards, plum and pear, branches bowed with almost-ripe fruit.

Abraham's moans grew louder. I knew he was marveling at the beauty, for our valley was indeed beautiful. Not all the world was beautiful. The year I turned seven, the year Mother died, I convinced Father to take me along on his travels. Had Father always gone alone on business like most of the men in our village, he'd never have even thought of taking me. But, like the Roman men, he brought his wife with him everywhere. It wasn't that he adopted Roman ways. It was just his own way: He wanted Mother by his side. I knew my presence on that journey would help to fill the void that Mother had left. Even at seven, I knew.

I traveled with Father southwest to Nazareth and then much further south to Jericho. I saw the red sands and the baked clay. I saw stony soil where only olive trees grew. I even saw date palms outside Jericho, though most of the date palms grew even further south in the great Ghor basin.

So I had learned that land could be barren or rich, ugly or beautiful. I looked around now with grateful eyes. Pride strengthened my step. In the valley here the trees stood so thick in spots that now, in midsummer, the sun could not penetrate between the leaves, such was the glory of this land.

It was midmorning by the time I lifted Abraham from the cart and helped him stretch out in the grass, protected from the searing summer sun by the shade of a plane tree.

I sat beside him. Abraham groaned and thrashed around until he was lying on his side. He looked at me.

My mind raced. Immediately I wished I hadn't brought him here. I hadn't been thinking clearly at all. What would happen if I had a fit while Abraham was here with me? He might tell.

The burden of secrecy was heavy. I was suddenly exhausted with it. People would find me out sooner or later. And I was already isolated —

by my own trips to the valley. What did it matter if Abraham told them?

Only I shouldn't have brought him along. What would happen to him if I had a fit and died here? He would starve to death. And starvation was the cruelest of deaths.

"I'm taking you home." I stood up.

"Sit down, Miriam." Abraham's voice was stern.

I sat. Abraham had never ordered me before. But it was his right: He was male and he was older. Yet the strangeness of this sudden turn of events confused me. My heart was loud in my ears. Abraham was the son of our servant.

He clutched my shift with his right hand, that hand that seemed to do part of his bidding. His hand was long and slender and white. My eyes moved from his hand to his face once more. If he were a girl, he would be beautiful. Only no one would see his beauty because he was twisted.

"Do whatever it is you do here. Ignore me."

I nodded. "All right." I gently unfastened his fingers from my shift. Then I stood and went to the nearest sycamore. I climbed high and sang. Every time I looked at Abraham, he seemed to be in a new position. He never looked comfortable, though. But he didn't call to me. He didn't seem to need me. I sang until my throat was hoarse. Finally, I climbed down.

Abraham didn't acknowledge my presence at his side for a long while. This was odd. The Abraham I knew, for all his lacks, was alert and aware. I scratched my arms restlessly. The tension between us mounted. I refused to be the first to speak. Incipient anger pecked at my neck. The boy was contrary.

"So this is meadow grass." Abraham plucked a blade with his right hand.

"You know meadow grass. Hannah and Father have taken you places. And Daniel did, before them."

"They never laid me on the ground."

So that was it. Abraham was angry with me! I stood up quickly. "I'm sorry. I thought you'd prefer it to the cart." I bent to lift him.

"I do. Sit, Miriam."

I sat on my heels, ready to jump up again.

"Is that mint over there?"

I went and picked him some leaves. "And

here's chamomile, as well." I added a few curls of the spice.

"And the yellow flowers?"

I smiled. "Dandelions. But they are nothing compared to what else grows here."

Abraham chewed on the mint leaves. "What else?"

"In the spring this meadow is strewn with red anemones."

"Spring is brief in Galilee."

"Brevity makes it that much more beautiful. The yellow jasmine winds through the trees behind us in such profusion you think they are the sun itself."

Abraham didn't answer.

"And that hill," I pointed, "the narcissus are so thick, you can't walk there without trampling them."

"You know the flowers by name."

"The herbs, too," I said, hearing my mother's voice come from my own mouth.

Abraham closed his eyes.

I waited. Then I cleared my throat. "Do you want to go home?"

He opened his eyes. "No." He looked at me and mischief crept into the smile lines around his mouth. "When you were singing before, I never heard anything like that. Do you imagine you're at a funeral?"

"A funeral?"

"The words are hardly appropriate for the dead, though you do wail them with sadness."

I tossed my hair over my shoulder. "I sing wherever and whenever I want." My voice was defiant, though I knew he was right. In Magdala the only place I had heard women sing was at funerals.

"Where did you learn the words?"

"I made them up."

Abraham laughed.

My cheeks went hot. "You're rude, which hardly becomes you. "

Now he laughed harder. "You have spirit, Miriam. And you sing well. But there are better songs to sing. Songs that heat the blood." Abraham rolled onto his back and looked up at the sky. "Do you want me to teach you the words?"

I scrambled to my knees and leaned over Abraham, hardly daring to believe what he'd just said.

"Would you?" He had scrolls with all the songs I yearned to know. He could do what he said. "Would you teach me?"

He smiled. "I'll do more than that. I'll teach you to read. Then you can read the songs whenever you like. You won't have to memorize them."

I sat back on my heels, stunned, my mouth open, my whole body tense. No women in our village read, not even the richest. There was no need to. The educated men kept the Torah and all the holy scriptures. They told the laborers and the servants and the women all that was necessary to know.

But I had heard of women elsewhere reading. Once I listened when Father came back from a pilgrimage to Jerusalem. He told Abraham of a woman scholar and teacher, whom people flocked to, just like they used to flock to the woman Huldah of centuries before. I had listened with wonder, but nothing more. I had never even dreamed of reading.

"Don't you want to?"

"Yes," I breathed. "Oh, yes."

"Then we will come here every day to this

very valley and you will introduce me to the plants of every season, each of them by name, and I will teach you to read."

As we went home, I didn't speak. My head spun. The world kept changing. A few months ago, I was one person, the person I had always been, the person I felt sure I would always be. Then the fit came, and I became the person who hid in the valley all day alone. And now I was different again — now I was going to learn to read.

Me. Miriam. A girl child from Magdala. A girl child who would read.

CHAPTER FOUR

I learned quickly. Partly because I was eager, but mostly because Abraham was a good teacher. Where I wanted immediate results and grew quickly frustrated, he was patient and ever encouraging, saying it would all come in good time. No one could have been a better teacher than Abraham.

I called him *peh rabboni* — teaching mouth — an unlovely and odd name, but one that suited him, for he was like the mouth of a rabbi, my own rabbi, my teacher and master. He liked it when I called him that.

We read together daily, always the songs, and always in private. Abraham said our reading wasn't secret, only private, just between us. He offered to help me read the Torah. We were the only family I knew of that had a Torah at home.

I never held it. Indeed, I had touched it on occasion, when I'd unroll it a bit for Abraham. But I never bore it in my hands. The idea made me anxious. Hannah never carried it either. It was always Father who placed the Torah before Abraham's hungry eyes.

So when Abraham spoke of the Torah, when he offered to teach me directly from the holy words, I shook my head and held out the scroll of songs instead. Not the *Song of Miriam* or the *Song of Deborah*, songs of women who were distant from me, whose words didn't stir the life within me, but the open passion of the *Song of Solomon*, the song called rightly the *Song of Songs*. Songs were what had made me dance when I was innocent, before my first fit. Songs were what made me still feel alive now. I could almost believe my breath was pure when it was transformed in a song.

As time went on, I knew I could unroll the *Song of Songs* whenever I wanted and read it at will. Yet I still worked to memorize the songs. If I knew a song with my eyes closed, it lived inside me. When I was at home, I padded in bare feet around the room, repeating the glorious words in a whisper to the bowls and table and stools, to the pillows and bed mats.

Whither is thy beloved gone, O thou fairest among women?

Who asked this question? And of whom was it asked? Hannah had begun to say that I was turning beautiful. She echoed Father. I wondered if anyone would ever consider me the fairest among women.

How beautiful are thy feet with shoes, O prince's daughter!

I wore shoes — at least, in the presence of all but our household I did — and sometimes, when I thought of how much Father and I had and how little Hannah and Abraham had, I did feel like a prince's daughter. Hannah promised that soon, very soon, she would weave me proper dresses. Hannah was as skilled a weaver as anyone. No shop in town carried better than Hannah could make herself. I fingered the soft, familiar cloth of my shift, which by now had faded to peachy pink. Shifts were for peasants and children. I was not a peasant and soon I would no longer be a child.

I sang even in my dreams and in those dreams I wore the womanly dresses Hannah had made for me and basked in the light of love from my beloved. But I never saw my beloved in my dreams. I never touched his hand. I never breathed his scent. I only heard his voice. A thin, keen voice that sang whatever I sang.

And, thus, my reading lessons and my knowledge of the canticles progressed, just as Abraham's knowledge of nature progressed. My only regret in these months was that Abraham was tone-deaf. He had heard all the canticles sung many times. Daniel used to take him regularly to the house of prayer, never failing to be there when the lesser clergy, the Levites, passed through town and sang. Abraham told me all about it. And Abraham had even heard the songs that belonged in the taverns. Someone had apparently taken him there, too. Abraham wouldn't tell me who. No one could ever accuse Abraham of being indiscreet. It was funny to me now that I had ever worried that Abraham might tell people if he saw me have a fit. He didn't talk to most people. He said they didn't care what he had to say, that most of them thought he was an idiot. I knew there was no idiocy in Abraham. And I knew, just as well, that there was not one note of musicality in him. Abraham had definitely heard all these songs, yet he couldn't teach me a single tune. And I desperately wanted to sing the songs the way they were meant to be sung. There were a couple I had heard at wedding festivities. But weddings were infrequent in a town so small as Magdala, and my memory didn't serve me well.

I tried guessing, singing first one way, then another, asking Abraham which sounded most right to him. But he laughed away my questions. Soon I stopped guessing because I knew his stone ear embarrassed him. Perhaps he wondered, as I did, whether it was connected to his paralysis.

So we passed the long, hot, dry months in songs, coming home to dine on the fruits and nuts we gathered. Abraham had always loved fruits and nuts. When he felt poorly and ate little, Hannah had the habit of coaxing his flickering appetite with fruits and nuts and, oh yes, honey — he sucked it right from the comb. But now his hunger for those foods was even stronger, augmented by the joy of seeing them growing, of telling me which to harvest for him.

One late afternoon as we were coming home from the valley, Abraham called out, "Pomegranates, Miriam."

I pushed on. There were no pomegranate trees around here. Shouldn't I have known? I was the one Mother taught to collect the bark for dye, after all.

"Stop."

I stopped the cart unwillingly. Father would be home soon, and we needed to beat him there. I walked around the cart and faced Abraham, ready to talk sense into him, when I saw the sure light in his eyes. I followed their gaze past the familiar bushes to a tree I hadn't noticed before, laden with fruit, the first pomegranates of the year. I pushed the cart hurriedly to it, then reached for a ripe one. It fell into my hand with the slightest tap.

"It's trying to jump to you, Abraham." I laughed. "It can't wait for me to take it home and peel it."

"Here." Abraham opened and closed the fingers of his right hand rapidly. "Let me hold it."

I put the smooth, thick-skinned ball in his hand and he turned it over and over. It was the perfect size for his fist. He turned it over so many times that it glistened with the oils of his skin. "Do you want me to peel it," I asked, "or do you intend to wear it away to the flesh?"

Abraham grinned. "Let's go home. Fast."

When we passed through the door, Hannah was out. I washed my hands and Abraham's, and we offered our thanks to the Creator. Then I fed him pomegranate, seed by seed. The juices ran down his pointed chin. I patted them away with a soft cloth.

"Stop." Abraham smiled with reddened teeth. "There won't be any left for you."

"We can pick more tomorrow." I pressed my lips together in satisfaction. "It's more fun to see how much you enjoy them."

"They're too wonderful to miss. I insist."

I loosened a seed and held it ready before my mouth. Plump, translucent. Abraham was right: They were too good to miss.

Suddenly Abraham jerked out his hand, grabbed my wrist, and pulled me toward him. He took the seed from my hand. "Come to me, Miriam." One by one, slowly and with great effort, he fed me the rest of the pomegranate.

His fingers were stained red for days afterward, as were mine.

Winter passed in whispered words and songs. A new spring came, and between tending the kitchen garden and reading with Abraham, I was almost entirely happy. Almost entirely satisfied. We wandered away the spring and summer and fall, the wheels of the cart growing thin, the soles of my feet growing calloused. We were as one.

It was well into the next winter before I had my second fit. I was close to twelve at that point and I felt older and wiser. The fit more than a year and a half before seemed so distant that sometimes I wondered if it had been the product of my child's imagination. The young woman I was now wouldn't have such flights of fancy.

The young woman I was now walked the solid earth and parted the little clouds of breath that preceded her down the street. She knew she was full of life.

I was with Abraham when it came. Naturally. We had not gone to the valley that day because of the qadim, the cutting dry east wind. It had come overnight and left the air clear as crystal and made the temperature plummet. The frozen bushes glittered; the trees reached toward the earth with icicle fingers.

Hannah was out when the fit came. At the well, of course, for there was nowhere else she ever went without Abraham other than the house of prayer, unless he was off with me in the valley. We were sitting by the fire. I loved the sort of day that justified a fire. Many of our neighbors had no fireplace inside their homes, but instead contented themselves with sitting around an open-air fire in their cooking lean-to. I was grateful for the luxury of our fireplace. The air smelled nutty, for we were burning the dead branches of pistachio trees.

I threw a log on, cheerful and unwary. Perhaps as cheerful as I had been that day in the valley when I sang of fawns, though never as light-hearted. Still, my body was infused with the intoxicating breath of the fire.

As the log left my hand, the bright light came; the flame of the fire split into a thousand sparks. The sweet smell of pistachio turned foul. A piercing scream cut the air. I wanted to shout. But no words came. It was as though a sheepskin had been placed over my face and I'd never breathe free again. Pain seared through my hand. My body was rock. Then I was pushed on my side.

In the instant that these things happened, my thoughts raced. My last fit had been no product of a child's feckless mind. A second demon had joined the first and I knew I was lost as the room went out of focus and I moved into a state of not knowing anything.

The water was icy on my cheeks.

I opened my eyes and cried out.

"Hush, child." Hannah cradled me in her arms. I struggled a moment, then settled against her cloak. The wool was rough and smelled of lanolin. I wondered irrelevantly why Hannah wore her cloak in the house, why she hadn't hung it on the peg by the door, but I was too tired to ask. Every muscle in my body was sore. I blinked my eyes. We were both on the floor by the fireplace. "You're safe now," Hannah crooned. "You're safe."

As the light in the room replaced the blackness that had filled my mind, I realized that I had fainted away, just as I had in my first fit. My right hand throbbed terribly. I held it up before my eyes. The blisters shone.

Hannah took my right wrist gently and dunked my hand into a bowl of water in which icicles floated. She held it there against my will till it grew numb and blue. Then she placed my hand on my stomach. "It will heal."

I twisted around and saw my friend pressed against the nearby wall, his eyes on my face. Worried eyes. "What happened?" I asked.

My words were directed at Abraham, but Hannah answered. "You leaned over and hit your head on the fireplace. Don't you remember?"

I kept my eyes on Abraham as Hannah spoke. I hadn't hit my head at all. Abraham knew that.

Hannah stroked my cheek. "You fell into the

fire and Abraham pushed you clear of danger. My Abraham." Hannah's voice trembled with pride. "Only your hand got burned. Only your hand."

Abraham had rescued me. It was he who pushed me on my side at the start of the fit.

Hannah put a cushion under my head and stood. "Your father should be told. If you feel well enough for me to leave now, I'll go for him." She reached for Abraham's poncho on the hook.

"Go," I said. "But leave Abraham here." I looked at Hannah. "I need him."

Hannah's eyes widened. "You need him?"

I had to talk to him alone. But I wouldn't explain to Hannah. Not now. "Leave him," I said with force. "I want him here."

My order seemed to relieve her. Wanting was more understandable than needing. "Yes, Miriam." She patted my shoulder gently and left.

I turned and faced Abraham. "Why did you lie?"

Abraham looked at me.

I got up, holding my wounded hand to my chest. I walked over slowly and sat beside him.

"It wasn't your first fit, was it?"

"My second."

Abraham's eyes wandered from my face. "I saw a boy have a fit once. Years ago. I was with your father. He took me to visit a healer who lived in a hut on the plain of Genezareth." Abraham paused. "It was hot and oppressive." He stopped, almost as though the memory made him tired. Then he turned his eyes back to me. "But the land was rich, farming land, and the green helped to make the heat bearable. I was breathing that heat. And so was the boy who came to be healed. Just like me. And he went rigid, thrashing stiff arms and legs. And he shook fast." Abraham's eyes were unmoving. He licked his lips. "Just like you."

I sidled closer. I hadn't known that I thrashed and shook, but of course that's what made me feel so exhausted. "What happened to him?"

"He opened his mouth wide."

I put my hands to the corners of my mouth, which still ached from stretching. I had opened my mouth wide like a snake. There were many poisonous snakes in our land, the asp, the horned viper, the adder. Was I full of toxins, or was

I merely a harmless colubrine that sneaked through the rocks and grasses? "What happened to him?"

"He spit and drooled. After that he made no more noise. His face turned blue, then dark purple. He stopped shaking." Abraham looked toward the fire. "He was dead."

I held my right hand, the burned hand, cupped in my left and rocked back and forth over it, my eyes closed. "Unclean."

"Nonsense."

I snapped my head up. "The boy was unclean. Unclean before death and unclean after."

"Why do you say that?"

"Why?" Was Abraham daft after all? "Everyone says that."

"Not everyone, only the stupid and thoughtless."

I stared at Abraham. "Where do you think illness comes from if not a lack of purity?"

"Are babies unclean, Miriam?"

"Babies? Of course not."

"I was born like this, Miriam. I was born with paralysis. I committed no sin."

But Abraham's father might have committed a sin and the sins of a father can be visited upon his child. Still, I couldn't say that to Abraham. In our household no one ever spoke of Abraham's father. "Job," I said slowly. "Maybe you are like Job. Maybe the Creator tests you."

"I have never questioned the Creator. I am not like Job." Abraham jerked his right hand out. "Look."

I took his hand and turned it over. "Teeth marks."

"Your teeth marks."

The marks were red and raw. I was mortified. "I bit you?"

"You foamed at the mouth and your teeth clenched. I remembered how the boy died years ago in Genezareth. I was afraid you'd stop breathing, like him. I was afraid you'd drown in your saliva. I pushed you until your head was sideways so that when your mouth opened again, the spit could pass. But my hand wasn't quick enough getting out of the way when you closed your jaws again. I believe I am lucky to have a hand at all."

I ran my fingers over the grooves in Abraham's hand. His words slowly began to make sense. "You helped me breathe."

"And you bit me." Abraham laughed. "Fine reward."

I dropped his hand and drew myself away from his laughter. What if I had really bitten his hand off — his right hand which was the only limb he controlled? These demons within me, these demons that could have stolen Abraham's one hold on the physical world, made me want to vomit — vomit and vomit until my retching turned me inside out and I was free of their evil. I was dangerous. And here Abraham was laughing. "But weren't you afraid of me? Weren't you afraid of the demons within me?"

Abraham laughed louder. "Demons. Is that who you're blaming for biting me?"

I shook my head hard. My eyes burned with the need to cry. "Don't you believe I'm a sinner? You may be one, too."

"Sinners?" Abraham sighed. "Oh, Miriam, I wish I could sin. But all I can do is watch."

I stared at him. "Envy," I said slowly.

"Yes." Abraham's voice was heavy and sad.

"Envy is a sin. Coveting is a sin." His eyes wandered once more. "Yes, I'm a sinner. But you're not, Miriam."

"I went into the valley alone. Women don't go alone."

"You didn't sin, Miriam. You broke no law of Moses and Israel. You're not sick because you sinned, Miriam. I'm not sick because I sinned. If there's anything I've figured out in my life, it's that invalids aren't any more sinners than anyone else."

Abraham's words sounded heretical. I was glad no one else was around to hear them. Yet I was equally glad that I had heard them. If the Torah didn't say that invalids were evil, then it didn't have to be so. And surely babies were not evil. Abraham might be right. How I wanted him to be right.

Perhaps his palsy, perhaps my fits, were just accidents of the body, like stomach pains that came and went, only that much more exaggerated. Maybe healers were the answer, after all. It might just be a matter of finding the right medicine. Something to be gained with searching and luck. I thought of all the herbs Mother had taught me about. "Abraham, do you know hyssop?"

"Hyssop and bignonia and polygonum and —"

"No, stop."

"We tried them, Miriam. Between my mother and Daniel, we tried every extract known. When I was small, I drank so many disgusting brews." Abraham's voice rose.

I couldn't bear it. I wouldn't bear it. There had to be something they hadn't tried. "Then a poultice — yes, a poultice of fish brine or . . ."

"The liver of a marten? Something simple." Abraham panted, as though out of breath. "Something simple, Miriam? Oh, no. There is nothing simple. Not for me, at least."

Nothing simple for Abraham. Nothing simple for me. No evil, yet still no escape. "Why?" The words came from deep in my throat, like a howl. "Why am I sick, Abraham? Why do I have fits?"

He looked at me.

I whispered, "Why us?"

"I don't know, Miriam. I don't think anyone knows but the Creator."

I moved still closer to Abraham, until our

shoulders touched. We sat side by side and looked into the fire. "Is there no hope for us?"

"If you mean, will things turn out well, will we be healed, I cannot answer. I doubt it for me. I cannot guess for you. But if you mean, will things make sense, then maybe, Miriam."

"Sense," I said. Maybe my fits made sense. I looked around at the stone walls of our house and I couldn't imagine how any of this made sense.

CHAPTER FIVE

Abraham and I argued. He said I should hide my fits. He said people didn't understand invalids, people were afraid of invalids, and if I revealed myself, I'd rue the day.

I said people could learn. I had learned.

Abraham laughed at me. He said necessity was a formidable teacher.

I raged against his warning. If Abraham were right and my fits were not the sign of demons, then I wanted everyone to know. I wanted the chance to face everyone and fight out the truth.

One summer night years before, when we slept on the flat roof to catch a bit of air because the khamsin wind from the desert scorched our tongues and throats, Father and a visiting friend sat hunched toward one another in fervent conversation. Father was counseling the man to confront a foe. Who or what, I couldn't catch. But the firmness of Father's voice, the absolute assurance of it, enveloped me as I drifted into sleep. In the morning the man was gone.

I now knew if I were to talk to Father openly, if Abraham would release me from the promise of secrecy just that much, Father would encourage me, just as he had encouraged that anguished man. I told Abraham that it was right that everyone should know who I was, that it was just for me to face them. I spoke what I knew Father would counsel.

But, despite my words to Abraham, I still harbored the fear that Abraham might be wrong about demons. I still wondered about the possibility of another life, an evil life, parasitic within me. And so my arguments with Abraham lacked conviction.

Eventually we compromised. I didn't tell Father or Hannah about the fits. I didn't tell anyone. But I no longer went to the valley daily. Instead, I went wherever I wanted, all about town or in the valley, as the mood dictated. And I pushed Abraham in the handcart with me everywhere. I went freely, never pausing to think what would happen if a fit struck right then. I almost wanted a fit to strike. Every step became a sort of challenge, a challenge that at once frightened me and drew me.

Abraham didn't agree to the compromise, but there was nothing he could do about it. I simply lugged him into the cart and off we went. And he loved going new places so much that he soon forgave my unfair tactics.

When we were in the valley, I collected herbs. I didn't hunt for them. Instead, I merely noticed what we passed and I tucked a bit of this, a bit of that into my cloth belt. That way the selection wasn't mine — that way I opened my heart and eyes to whatever path the Creator might set me on. It was an act of faith. I scraped bark with the knife I kept in that belt. I plucked the small, fragrant leaves from stems with the sure fingers of my mother. I was a daughter of a woman, though she was dead. I was a daughter surrendering myself to the power of good. Abraham didn't say anything, but he saw what I did.

Once when I dug up a mandrake root, he insisted on carrying it the rest of the day. He held the root, forked and fleshy, in his right hand and said it was the hips and thighs of his true love. He laughed, but I stared and heat climbed my cheeks and reverberated in my ears. The mandrake resembled a woman's body, there was no doubt about it.

In the mornings when Hannah was milling or spinning flax, after we had washed the clothes, after I had tended the kitchen garden, I made a strong healing brew from the herbs I'd collected the day before. Abraham and I drank it in silence. I knew he put no hopes in the brew; I knew he thought of the futile brews of his childhood. Yet he was kind: He never refused to take his sips, he never again suggested there was no point. We drank without fail.

And not from just any gray clay cup. I stirred each new brew in the little red pitcher whose black swirls had laughed at me when Mother used to pour from it. And I carefully measured out the liquid into the two yellow bowls with fine ribs of red. I had planned to take them with me when I married. But now I used them daily with Abraham. We drank. Then we went out to meet the world.

Abraham delighted in every moment outside

our home. He especially loved going to the market at the foot of the high tower that our town was named after. We went on the second and fifth days of the week, without fail.

The birds attracted him the most, the partridge and quail that the rich ate, the ducks and geese, even the cheap and plentiful pigeons. We sat among the animals, the weaned kid or lamb, the fatted calf. The animals paid us no mind. We were as though invisible. I knew that Abraham loved the animals for that. It was a respite.

But I would never allow us to stay there too long. I had to be among people. I had to put us on display. I was ready for whatever would happen. Ready for the next fit. I would speak to the moment. That was my decision, arrived at after feeling the eyes of the villagers on our backs day after day, week after week. Oh, yes. I would enlighten the village about illness.

So I pushed the cart through the market crowds with purpose, and Abraham and I marveled at the piles of carp and scaleless catfish from our own Sea of Galilee, and we were proud when buyers came from out of town to take barrels of our muries, the salted fish that made the name of Magdala known as far as Rome. We wandered through the stacks of melons, figs, olives, the piles of wheat and barley and rice and four different kinds of locusts, weaving our way among all the burdened, braying donkeys. It seemed everyone in the world owned at least one donkey. Abraham loved the whole confused mess. And I welcomed it. I welcomed every chance to stand among all those people. My eyes were alert for the flash of light that signaled a coming fit. I was ready.

But, as it turned out, I had prepared myself for the wrong thing.

One morning a Roman foot soldier passing through town stopped near us in the market as we marveled at the exotic foods crowded together on the spread-out cloth of a traveling peddler from the north. The Roman laughed at our round eyes — for that's what Abraham and I were in those days, just eyes observing the world, me from behind my veil and Abraham from the shell of his cart — and the Roman said, in accented Hebrew, that we hadn't seen anything until we'd seen the great market in

Jerusalem. I'd never been addressed by a Roman before. I'd never talked to any pagan ever, nor even to a man of Israel that wasn't known to my Father. We didn't dare answer him, though questions crowded in our mouths.

But our silence didn't deter him. He told us of hens' eggs that the Romans prepared in so many ways. He told us of the meat of deer and gazelle that graced the tables of kings. He made our mouths salivate with descriptions of the dates from Jericho.

He took an apple from the top of the pile, an apple from Sodom, and ate loudly. Its sweet juice perfumed the air and made his bottom lip shine. Our people never stood as they ate. There was something about this act of eating standing, without a prayer, that put me on edge. I was aware of how his sweat-stained shirt stuck to his chest. I was aware of the coarse black hair on the back of his hands. A vague anxiety made me stand tall and alert, my chin pointing forward, not down.

So when this Roman man cocked his head and spoke again, it was as though I had braced myself for what he was about to say. Still, the words jolted me. "The cripple will never see Jerusalem. But you might, little lady. With some rouge and nard, I can see you making a bed in Jerusalem, so to speak." And he laughed again.

We left quickly, for I knew what he meant. The women of Israel loved their scents and ornaments. But he had not spoken to me as a proper woman of Israel, adorning herself for her husband. I knew, and so did Abraham.

A sick feeling settled in my stomach and wouldn't leave. Prostitutes gave up their souls to false gods; they were bestial. I knew the story of the daughter of a priest who turned to whoredom and was burned for her sin. My skin crawled with the horror of burning, a sentence that went so against the law of nature. I was not bestial — a wild dog — nor would ever be. I was an Israelite forever.

It was more than a month before I returned to the market, and then I steered clear of apples.

Later Abraham swore to me that when Daniel finally came back from Alexandria, he would get him to take us both to Jerusalem. I didn't answer.

I knew I could get Father to take me to Jerusalem if I asked, but I knew he wouldn't take Abraham along. It was one thing to have an invalid in the house with Hannah servicing him; it was quite another to think of traveling afar with that invalid.

Would Daniel really take Abraham to Jerusalem? It had been so long since we'd received word of Daniel that I was beginning to doubt he'd ever return. But if he did and if he agreed to take us to Jerusalem, would Father entrust me to Daniel? What would the villagers say?

The Roman had taught me much. The villagers' nervous eyes following us in the market now meant different things to me. They posed a new challenge.

No other decent woman walked freely through the streets, going wherever she wanted with no fixed purpose. Decent women went about their house chores or ran shops. They sold textiles, incense, clothing. They worked at the glassblowers' and made bottles. From their doors they sold olives and braided breads. They worked in the fields in groups of three or more, never alone. They walked to the house of prayer, but only when the streets were almost empty, only when market time was nearly over. The only people who wandered about the market in our town were men buying and selling, and beggars, and prostitutes.

No other cripples were pushed in carts through the midst of crowds. Cripples sat in one place, calling out relentlessly for alms and food.

No other couple was like Miriam and Abraham.

Hannah had been alarmed from the very first. She said the villagers talked about me and Abraham. She feared that if I became an issue because of Abraham, Father would cast her out. At the time I had thought her fears foolish. I didn't understand what she meant. Not completely. Not until the Roman foot soldier.

But Father also hadn't seemed to give full weight to Hannah's fears. He had quelled them, saying Abraham could never be the cause of problems for our household. He was overcome with gratitude toward Abraham for saving me from the fire. I was all Father had in this world. He told everyone of Abraham's heroics. They listened and nodded, their faces speaking sympathy.

Oh, Father was confused the first time I passed him on the streets, bumping along with Abraham, that third day of our public wanderings. "Miriam, where are you going?" His hands were open, almost as though he expected me to fall into them, as though I must be in need of great physical support.

I smiled at him, pleased to have happened upon him so soon and so naturally. Pleased to have him know what I was doing without my having had to design a meeting. "Anywhere, Father. Everywhere. We want to see everything."

He pursed his lips. "You're not on an errand?" His brow crinkled with irritation. "Doesn't Hannah need your help at home?"

"I fetched the water for her before we left. I scrubbed the laundry and hung it. I'll be home in time to help with the evening meal."

"There's more to running a household than the daily laundry and meals."

"I know that, Father. I help in every way I can.

But the day is long. It's so much more interesting being out and about." My eyes pleaded with his.

Father didn't look convinced. "You could sew, embroider, something. Jewish women keep their hands busy."

"I'm no better at sewing than Mother was."

My words came spontaneously, but they worked like the best laid plan, for Father nodded slowly. "Your mother liked adventure." He let his outstretched hands fall to his sides. "She traveled with me everywhere. She didn't care to stay behind and keep the house in my absence." His voice grew more tender as he talked.

"I know, Father. I remember."

"You look more like your mother every day." Sadness colored his face. But then he shook his head, as though to free it from the memories we shared. "I don't like you walking alone through the village, Miriam."

"I'm not alone, Father." I smiled at Abraham.

Father looked at Abraham and hesitated. Then he nodded resolutely. "Be attentive, Miriam and Abraham." He leaned over Abraham. "You saved her from the fire once. But it's wiser to keep clear of fires." He straightened up and looked at me as though examining me. "You are old enough to wear a veil, Miriam." His voice turned slightly harsh.

"You're right, Father."

"You must close that lovely face of yours behind the two kerchiefs."

"Yes, Father."

"Leave only one eye free, to see your path."

I bit my bottom lip. This was how Hannah wore her veil when she visited the shops. It was not required by law or custom. It was another of Hannah's mysterious extra rules, like the banning of purple. "Yes, Father."

"And you must plait your hair and keep it hidden."

"I'll do that, Father. Not a single strand of hair will show."

Father's face softened. "Hannah can help you put ribbons and bows on the forehead band."

"Yes, Father," I said, though I had no interest in ribbons and bows. I had given up decoration after my first fit. I would be content, in fact, to wear a simple headcloth, not a veil at all. But in public a veil would be more suited, I knew.

Father nodded, calm now.

He looked so satisfied, that I dared to speak up. "And if the veil should come a little jostled now and then, so both eyes can see the world, that wouldn't be too awful, would it, Father?"

Father looked surprised. Then he smiled. "You are my joy, Miriam." He touched Abraham's shoulder. And he left. After that he waved to us heartily whenever he saw us in the streets, even from a distance. My love for Father swelled. And after that it didn't bother me one whit not telling him about the fits, for I knew they wouldn't matter to him. The Creator may have blighted me with fits, but He had blessed me, as well; no other man was like Father.

Now remembering Father's words and smile, I was amazed. He thought a veil could protect me. I had donned that veil obediently; I was wearing it when the Roman foot soldier talked to me. I admit I had let it slip open so that both eyes showed. I admit that with my chin thrust forward like that, the curves of my face were apparent through the veil. But I had done nothing to suggest a lack of virtue. Nothing but be where decent women didn't go.

Father thought there was magic in a veil; he thought it was so simple. My father. Did Hannah and I know more of the world than Father did?

But I would not let my newfound knowledge stop me. I would rise to the challenge of the nervous eyes that followed me. I had a right to walk the streets of my own village. If any man were to address me again as the Roman foot soldier had, I would not run. I would speak up. Even to a stranger.

But would I really? Could I?

CHAPTER SIX

The last few months until my twelfth birthday passed and I did not find out whether or not I had the courage to speak up in my own defense. For no man ever did address me as the Roman foot soldier had. Not then, nor in the next year, either. And eventually the tension in my shoulders eased. Eventually the veil that covered one eye at all times (for, as I grew older, Hannah's zealous rituals seemed sensible to me) slipped open and my fingers didn't rush to clutch it closed immediately. Eventually I could look at apples without a pounding in my chest, though I didn't eat them at our table anymore.

I pushed Abraham's cart with an almost light heart once more. The days were filled with unremarkable acts. I learned to give thanks for the ordinary moments of daily life.

The only noteworthy event of that time was the coming of my blood. I had worried about the mikvah. I don't know why. Every woman went. Every man or child who wanted to be cleansed of something went. But I had avoided it since Mother died. The last time I had gone, the only time, was after her funeral, for I had insisted on holding her hand while the women prepared her body for burial. Those who touch the dead are unclean. I needed that uncleanliness. I helped wrap Mother in the shroud. I walked with the women before her bier. I cried with the flutes. And after that I went regularly to her grave, for she was buried on our own property, near the terebinth tree whose penetrating scent she claimed could cleanse the very soul. I knew of no one else buried near a terebinth. And I knew there were women in town who thought the burial spot a scandal.

I used to wonder about that. But now that I knew scandal in a new way, now that I myself was a topic for whispers, I took pleasure in that gravesite. I felt closer to Mother, as though we shared a secret gift that others mistakenly believed a flaw. And witness to their mistake was the family of doves that raised their brood there as the tree leafed out each spring.

Now I went to the mikvah regularly, as well — once each month. I walked across town to the baths after sunset. There I descended the stone steps completely free of garments. Women shed everything, including rings, necklaces, earrings. I wore no jewelry. So all I had to doff was my veil, my shift, my underclothes, and sandals. I entered the water covered only with the goose bumps that came from anticipation. I immersed myself deep, until the very tips of my long loose hair finally surrendered their attachment to the surface of the water and sank below with the rest of me. I hurried home feeling light and happy and grateful just for being alive.

During the days my blood flowed, I did not walk around town or in the valley with Abraham. I read beside him in the house. But when I came home from the mikvah every month, I gathered Abraham into his cart and we went about our way until the next blood came. Life had rhythm.

Only once was this happy rhythm interrupted. Abraham had taken an interest in carpentry. There were two furniture makers in town, Caleb and Shiphrah's husband Jacob. Jacob had the larger shop, large enough for Abraham and me to find a spot in a corner where we could sit and watch.

Jacob was a successful businessman. Maybe more successful than Father. Shiphrah's arms were spangled with jewelry. And three full-grown men were employed as helpers in Jacob's shop. People said that if you wanted something special, if you had a task that required true skill, then Jacob's was the only shop to go to.

We sat silent as the workers made everything from an infant's cradle to a roof parapet. Abraham watched attentively and later he would explain to me why they'd cut the notch just so or what made them reject one piece of wood in favor of another. He delighted in understanding the process.

Jacob's shop became our first stop of the day. And it started our day right, until the morning when Jacob came into the shop late. His face was ruddy with excitement and he looked angry. I had heard the workers talk amongst themselves before of Jacob's bad days. I should have remembered their words then.

Jacob's helpers had already started in on the tasks they'd been working on the day before. They hardly looked up when he entered. In retrospect it was clear they didn't want to acknowledge his mood and thus, perhaps, fan his anger. There were clues all around me, if only I had given them their due, for Jacob never forgave me that day's error.

Jacob stomped over to the pieces of wood for the cabinet he was building. He picked up a board and set it on a table. He measured it with a cubit and prepared to cut.

Abraham quickly grabbed my sleeve. I leaned my ear close to his lips. He whispered, "Stop him, Miriam. He's used the wrong measurement."

I'd never spoken to Jacob before. A woman didn't address a man needlessly outside the home, even a man who knew her husband or father, as Jacob knew mine. But this wasn't needless. I had to speak before Jacob cut the board through and wasted it. I cleared my throat. "May I speak?"

All four men looked at me, their faces amazed.

I flushed behind my veil and spoke loudly. "Are you sure that's the right measurement?"

Jacob put down his tool and crossed his arms at the chest. "What did you say?" His face was grim.

I panicked. I leaned toward Abraham. "Are you sure?"

"That piece is to go into the back," hissed Abraham in my ear. "It has to be longer."

"Isn't that the piece for the back?" I pointed. "Shouldn't it be longer?"

"That's right." One of the helpers nodded. "The cripple told her."

Jacob spun around and faced his helper. For a moment I thought they would fight. Over what? What offense had Jacob taken? But I didn't wait to find out. I tugged on Abraham and got him into his cart.

Jacob turned back to us. "No idiot can come in here and tell me what to do. Get out!" He was shouting now. "Out!" He lifted his thick arm in threat. But we were already backing out the door.

I raced through the streets, bumping the cart along as fast as I could. I was angry and frightened and angry at being frightened. This was worse than the Roman foot soldier. Much worse. No one had threatened us before. Oh, only a few had ever been friendly. But the others had either pretended to ignore us or, at the worst, avoided us. I had come to believe that Abraham and I were accepted — an oddity, still, but an accepted oddity. How stupid I was.

I seethed at Jacob's words and actions. Abraham didn't speak as I let all my feelings pour out. Then he simply said we shouldn't go back to Jacob's shop ever again. It was a finished matter, as far as he was concerned.

But it wasn't finished. Not for me. I had fled the Roman foot soldier in silence. And I had fled Jacob in silence. Yes, his raised arm was heavy as a club. But there were three other men in his shop. If I had stood my ground, they would never have let him strike us. And even if they had, wouldn't that have been better than fleeing? Fleeing, as though we were the ones who had wronged. Fleeing, as though we were the ones in shame. In that flight I had failed myself — I had gone against all that I had decided after the Roman foot soldier. I sat on the floor at home and counted the beats of my heart, and with each beat I promised myself that the next time, the very next time, I would not be silenced. This matter was not finished in my heart.

And, no, it wasn't finished for Jacob, either. He came to our home that night. And Father stood before him in the doorway.

"Welcome to my home, Jacob." Father moved to give his guest the customary welcome kiss.

Jacob jerked his head away. "Keep the cripple far from my shop."

Father stepped back. I waited for him to turn questioning eyes to me — reproachful eyes — for I had not told him of what passed in the carpenter's shop. This was my battle, not Father's.

But Father didn't look at me. He swept his hand back as if to bid Jacob enter. "Did something happen, Jacob? Come in and talk."

Jacob remained in the doorway. "Keep him away. I don't want an idiot hanging around my shop."

Father lifted his chin. I thought of how I had lifted my chin to the Roman foot soldier. I had learned that from Father, I realized. I could sense him bristle and I watched closely. This was what else I had to learn: how to speak up.

"Abraham is not an idiot." Father's voice was soft, but clear. "And even if he were, we should show him generosity and justice, true charity. Magdala is a small town, Jacob. It is easy to know one another. Surely we can find it in our hearts to accept our neighbors."

"Magdala is a strong town. It is not a town for idiots and cripples. Listen to our Jewish leaders."

Father clenched his jaw and the hairs of his whiskers moved. "Jewish leaders? Leaders are those whose wisdom earns our ear. Have you not heard the words of Hillel? 'What is hateful to you, do not to your neighbor.'"

"Idiots and cripples would not be my neighbors if people like you didn't harbor them."

"Idiots and cripples will always be with us, Jacob. They are part of life. They come from loins like mine and yours."

"Not mine! Defend your accusation!"

My mouth went dry. I thought of Jacob and Shiphrah's baby daughter, whom the traveling exorcist had failed to save more than three years ago. Had she lived, would she have been crippled?

But Father shook his head. "Taking offense where it's not intended won't change things, Jacob. Nor will pretending to misunderstand. You know what is as well as I do. Cripples are part of humanity. Take Hillel into your heart."

"You sound like a Pharisee." Jacob's top lip lifted slightly to show the tips of his teeth in a smirk. "And you're the one who had that Zealot Daniel hanging about all the time. Don't think I don't remember. You give yourself airs."

"I am a common Jew, like you, Jacob. I am trying to live a just and pious life, like you."

"You shouldn't keep him in your house. You shouldn't let your daughter walk the streets."

"It's no concern of yours who lives in this home." I had never heard Father raise his voice, but now that voice trembled. I knew he fought the urge to shout. "It's no concern of yours what my daughter does."

"It's everyone's concern when you don't live like the rest of us."

"Jacob, we don't all live alike. Open your eyes. We share this world with many, many who are less fortunate than you or I." Father gripped the edge of the door with one hand. "But you need not share any of your shop with Abraham and Miriam. Go now. They will never cross your threshold again." Father closed the door in Jacob's face.

I ran to Father and threw my arms around his chest.

But he peeled me away from him. "Listen well." He spoke slowly and decisively, as though his words were the Creator's law. Yet the tremble was still there. "I disapprove of your actions. Time should be spent in service, not in searchings or pleasures or whatever else it is that draws you. I should have stopped you, Miriam, two years back, when you started these wanderings into town. When you were still a child, under my guidance." Father laced his fingers together tightly. "Miriam and Abraham, if you are to govern your own actions, if you are to make your own path through this life, then you must be responsible for each step you take. Jacob's lone voice spoke today. But when one voice speaks, scores of others are in silent agreement. They don't understand you. I don't understand you."

He sighed. "I made a promise to Jacob tonight. See that my promise is kept, for your sake. Let caution guide your feet."

He looked down in silence for a moment. When he looked up again, he turned to the shelf, reaching for his tallith. But there was no need — for I held it ready in my hands. He dipped his fingers in the always ready bowl and sprinkled water on both forearms. I bowed and the fringes that ran the length of the shawl kissed my cheeks as Father threw it over his head and shoulders, those fringes without which the tallith would be unfit for its purpose.

We never did go to Jacob's shop again. We never even walked down the street his shop was on. As Father had said to Abraham, it was wiser to keep clear of fires.

CHAPTER SEVEN

It wasn't until several months after my thirteenth birthday that another fit came, a fit I believe I brought on myself.

Hannah had woven me a long dress with many colored stripes the year before, the kind of dress I would have delighted in wearing when I was younger, the kind of dress that made a young woman feel beautiful. It had pleats, a style that had only recently come to Magdala. I admired the dress, but I had no desire to wear it. I wasn't going to marry, so beauty didn't matter.

I had come to the decision not to marry purely by logic. First, it was likely that a fit would come while I was in public, for I spent much of my day in public. And if a fit came, no man would marry me. Even if I had the good fortune to convince others that fits were not the sign of demons, they would only be convinced with their heads, not with their hearts. Jacob the carpenter had taught me this. In his head he knew Abraham was intelligent; how could he not, after Abraham had corrected him? Yet he was resolute in casting Abraham as an idiot. There was no reason to expect any different reaction toward me once people discovered my fits. So no one would marry me. How could a sane man risk taking a woman who might be the vessel of evil into his home to bear his children?

And if by chance my fits did not make themselves known to others, I still would not marry. For I was unwilling to keep a secret from my husband. Love between man and woman should be complete, with neither holding back from the other. If there was anything I owed to the memory of Mother, it was the belief in love that she had murmured to me as she plaited my hair or soothed me to sleep. Belief in a perfect love. Now an impossible love.

So I saw no reason to wear the dress Hannah had made for me, though I assured her it was lovely, as lovely as any girl could have wanted. The dress sat in a basket, unused for over a year.

Hannah seemed to accept my decision. I believe she had come to the conclusion that I was hard-headed and that there was no fighting it. She backed off quickly whenever we disagreed on even the smallest matters.

She backed off like that until the one warm evening when I came home with Abraham, only to see Judith leaving our home in a hurry. I was blissful that night. After the encounter with Jacob, I thought I might never be blissful again. But time passed and, with its uneventfulness, the memory dulled and my resilient spirit once more reached for the pleasures of this world.

Yes, that evening I was heady with the aroma of the roses a merchant had been selling in the market. Roses from Jericho. I'd never seen a rose before. A petal had landed heavily on my foot and I stooped to touch it. The thick sponginess so surprised me that I quickly rubbed the petal on Abraham's ankle, dangling from the cart. So he, too, knew the rose's flesh. Then I let it fall again.

I thought of the market after nightfall, the beggars roaming through on the lookout for wayward vegetables. I imagined a beggar woman coming across this petal, rubbing it between thumb and forefinger, for an instant enveloped in the luxury of the rose, for an instant blissful like me.

The sight of Judith ruptured that image. Judith acted as though she hadn't seen me, but I had the sensation that she was avoiding me. Vague apprehension replaced the finely outlined vision of the rose.

I carried Abraham through the door, draped over one shoulder. He had grown, of course, lengthened out like a palm frond. But I also had grown. I was perhaps the tallest female in all Magdala, though Father said the old woman Martha had stood taller than me in her youth. Now Martha was so bent it was hard to think of her as tall. I had grown strong, as well. Pushing the handcart, even with Abraham's lightness, had built up the muscles of my arms and calves. I couldn't imagine feeling healthier — and I recognized the irony of that thought. I never forgot my fits.

No sooner had I closed the door behind me than Hannah began. "Miriam, we need to talk."

I placed Abraham in the middle of the pillows Hannah and I had made him years ago and sat on the floor beside him. I looked at Hannah expectantly.

She hesitated. She ran her tongue across her top teeth. Then she got up and fetched the basket with the dress. "I'd like you to wear this."

"Is there a special event coming up?" Passover was behind us, but perhaps a wedding was coming. I had not gone to a wedding since the onset of my fits. I wanted to go when Deborah got married. And it grieved me to stay at home when Sarah celebrated her union. But though I was no longer trying to conceal my fits by then, I couldn't bear the thought of possibly convulsing in the middle of a wedding feast, of soiling the celebration of what I ached for — the love between man and woman.

I thought now of the young girls of the town. Who could it be that Hannah spoke of? Who was of age? I had gone my way with Abraham for so long now, it was as though no one else existed. Did I miss the company of those girls? Maybe it was time for me to risk a wedding. I could stay on the outskirts of the crowds, in the shadows. I could watch the dancing. "Is someone getting married?"

"You should get married, Miriam."

My heart clutched. Was this why Judith had come visiting? "Has a marriage been arranged? That's not right." I stood up. "Hannah, I'm too old for an arranged marriage. And Father promised Mother I would never have to marry someone I didn't love."

"No one has arranged a marriage, Miriam. But you are thirteen now. Almost fourteen. You are fully grown. It's time for you to dress like a woman of your class. It's time for you to appear as the sort of young woman a man would want as the mother for his children."

"Thank the Lord!" I said without thinking. "No match has been made." I sank back to the floor.

"Miriam!" Hannah's face was aghast. "What has possessed you? Don't you want to marry?"

"No."

"Miriam!" Hannah put down the basket and sat beside me. She took my right hand, the one with the scars from the fire years before. "Miriam, you must take a husband."

I looked at her and spoke words that Hannah least of all could deny. "Not all women get married, Hannah."

"Not all, no." Hannah didn't flinch. I was glad; I hadn't meant to hurt her. I'd meant only to stop her. She didn't stop, though. She said firmly, "But almost all." I pulled my hand back, but she held on and squeezed. "Miriam, the Creator put man on this earth to be fruitful and multiply. Every man should have at least two children, one to replace himself and one to multiply. This is a commandment. It is law. You do not have to follow that commandment. This law is made for man, not woman. But, think, Miriam. How can men do that if women stay celibate?"

"There is no shortage of women in our town."

Hannah nodded. "No. And no shortage of men, either. All our women are needed."

"I have no suitors, Hannah."

"But you would, Miriam. You would if you'd act as though you'd receive one."

I looked away from her.

"What is it? Miriam, tell me."

I stared at the wall. "The dress you made will be too small by now. I've grown, Hannah. I keep growing. Maybe I'll never stop."

"Is that all it is? I made the dress with a deep hem. I can have it the right size by the time you wake tomorrow. And there are tall men, Miriam. If you want help finding a tall husband, we can ask for help."

"That's why Judith came, isn't it?"

Hannah patted my hand, as though I were a child. "She has been patient these many years. It's time for her to come into your father's bed as his wife."

"Father could marry her any time he liked. So he must not want to. It has nothing to do with whether I stay here or not."

"It has everything to do with you, Miriam. Your father adores you. He knows you dislike Judith. Every time he's mentioned her to you, you've shown your feelings."

"That's nonsense. If he wanted to marry her, he would."

"Your father told Judith he will marry her as soon as you are married."

I shook my head in disbelief. Father couldn't love Judith. And he would never marry without love. Nor would I. "I won't take a husband."

"Miriam, be sensible." Again Hannah squeezed my hand gently. "You have so much love to give. You will be a wonderful wife, a wonderful mother. Wear the dress. Act like other girls your age and a match will come."

Hannah's words sliced cleanly through my heart. What wouldn't I give to be truly like other girls my age? I wanted a husband to sing to me, to sing,

Stay me with flagons, comfort me with apples; for I am sick from love.

The second canticle rang in my ears. I wanted a husband delirious with love for me. I wanted to be equally delirious. But my wants counted for nothing. Tears welled and spilled down my cheeks.

I looked at Hannah's hopeful face. I had to help her feel that my not marrying was best. "Hannah, if Judith marries Father, you will be her servant." I stopped and brushed the tears from my cheeks with my free hand. It was difficult to talk but there was no need to say more, anyway. Judith was bossy by nature. She had no servants now — and I was sure she'd revel in her power over having one.

"Judith is a good woman." Hannah's lips came together primly. She would not dare speak ill of her future mistress.

I swallowed and found my voice again. "Would she let Abraham stay here with you?" I watched Hannah's face close, masking all expression. I pressed on. "Have you asked her?"

"I haven't asked." Hannah let go of my hand and folded her own hands in her lap. "Miriam, if you would take us, Abraham and I would come with you to your new home. You would not have to mill or bake or wash."

I looked at Abraham. He had thrown himself backward in the pillows. I couldn't see his face. I knew he didn't want me to see his face. "Other men are not like Father, Hannah. We know that. A husband might refuse. His parents might refuse. And I would have no power to insist."

Hannah shook her head. "Don't do this,

Miriam. Don't make me fear your getting married. It is best for you that you marry. I must encourage you to marry." She shoved the basket in front of me. "I'll lengthen the dress tonight. Wear it, Miriam. Please."

"Where? It would get ruined, the way Abraham and I go about all day."

"Don't go all over town. It's not right, Miriam. Go to the house of prayer tomorrow."

"The house of prayer?" In all my years, I had not entered the house of prayer. Hannah knew that. "But why?"

"The Levites will be there. Abraham has told me you love the canticles and the psalms. They'll be singing the psalms. They may even sing from the *Song of Songs*. Go, and let the men of Magdala see your devotion."

The canticles. For so long I had hungered to hear them sung the right way. And just a moment ago I had considered even going to a wedding in order to hear them. But the house of prayer was sitting there, waiting, the whole time. The house of prayer was much less of a threat than a wedding. If I had a fit, who would I disgrace? The Creator had already seen my fits.

The Levites might sing things that meant nothing to me. They might sing only the psalms about war and righteousness, about confusion and judgments. But, oh, they might sing about love. And, yes, oh, yes, I'd go to the house of prayer in the fancy dress. "I'll take Abraham and we can —"

"Go without Abraham."

"No." The idea was unthinkable. Why, Abraham would delight in the songs as much as I would.

Hannah looked at Abraham. "Tell her, Abraham. Tell her to leave you behind."

Abraham worked to roll to one side so he could look at us. "Miriam is finding her own sense in life, Mother. I can no more change her future than a leaf can refuse to fall from the tree."

I stood up and spoke eagerly. "Let's measure the dress, Hannah. I'll wear it when I go to the house of prayer with Abraham tomorrow."

Hannah pressed her lips together. Then she did as I asked. She did as expected.

Hannah and Judith and Sarah and all the women I knew — they did as expected. And tomorrow I would go to the house of prayer and for one day I, too, would do as expected.

The next day we went. Hannah put a new veil across my face and with the dress on I wondered if anyone we passed would know who I was. But no one else pushed a cripple in a handcart, so I needn't have wondered.

I got there early and parked the handcart beside the entrance. I carefully took off Abraham's shoes and my own and set them in the cart. The stone steps of the house of prayer were smooth with wear. Their steepness scooped in the middle from all the passing feet. I asked for help and two women I could not identify behind their veils worked with me to carry Abraham up and in. We took our place at the side. Abraham sat on the floor, propped against the wall.

The people came in slowly. Some of them glanced at us and nodded. Others glanced and quickly looked away.

The service began. The men prayed aloud. The women remained silent, their eyes lowered. I stayed very still, as well. I listened closely to the words. Prayer after prayer, each one strong and glowing. I wanted to memorize every word:

> *Blessed be Thou, O Lord our God, King of the Universe . . .*

I was hot with the joy of being a Jew, a child of the King of the Universe. I closed my eyes in reverence. The prayer went on:

> *who has not made me a Gentile . . .*

and, yes, I was grateful I was not born pagan,

> *who has not made me a slave . . .*

and, yes, I was grateful I had not lived centuries ago when Israel suffered under the hands of the Egyptians,

> *who has not made me a woman.*

My eyes flew open. Surely the men had made a terrible mistake. Everyone would be demanding they start this prayer over. I looked around. But no one seemed upset. I turned to Abraham. He watched me, his eyes alert, as though he, too, expected something to happen.

The prayers went on. Men's voices in unison, but the words blended for me now, like the distant roll of thunder preceding the rains that overflowed the Sea of Galilee in early spring and again in fall.

And then the women were reciting their own prayers, and I wasn't even listening to them. I couldn't hear anything outside my own head.

The Creator had made me a woman. Should I be sad? Were all these women sad? Did they know something I didn't know? Something that every mother taught her daughter but that my mother had overlooked telling me? Or perhaps I'd been too young when Mother died for her to tell me. And I wasn't Hannah's daughter, after all. It wasn't her duty to tell me.

The men had thanked the Creator for not making them women. Their words echoed in my head.

These were the words of the prayer service. Holy words. I should have asked Abraham to teach me as much from the scriptures as he was willing. I shouldn't have insisted on learning only the songs. Did the Torah explain why men should be grateful they weren't women? But, surely, I could figure out the answer myself, even without the help of a mother.

Women had the joy of raising children, but they also had uncleanliness every month when their blood came and they had the pain of childbirth. That must have been what the men were grateful for — that they would have no blood, no pain. Yes, it was right. The Creator made men and the Creator made women, and we all owed gratitude for the way we'd been made. A woman should be as grateful she hadn't been made a man as a man was grateful he hadn't been made a woman. For a man could never know the pleasures of motherhood. And while I, too, would never know the pleasures of motherhood, it was by my own choice. The Creator had granted me the power to give birth. I should be grateful for that gift. And for the gift of my wise father and gentle Hannah and mentor Abraham.

Now I was able to listen again. The Levites'

voices filled the air. They sang of clapping hands and triumphant shouts in praise of the King of the earth. They sang of mercy and blessings and fear. And then, oh truly merciful Lord, they sang the beautiful songs of love. It was so unlikely after their first songs. As unlikely as Mother's insistence on love. The men sang the fourth canticle, the canticle I thought of as the canticle of the fawns, that canticle I first talked about with Father, my favorite of all canticles. I concentrated. And, yes, finally, I understood the love in this canticle not just as love between man and woman as they unite, but between the Creator and His people, our Israel. It was a charmed moment, a moment that comes but rarely. Oh, I knew these words in my sleep. The melody repeated itself. It was easy to learn. And I was opening my mouth now and I was singing. I sang the words I'd sung so many times before, but now I sang them to their rightful tune. I sang all the love in my heart.

Suddenly I realized my voice was alone. I sang, but no one else did. The Levites had stopped. The men, who stood at the front, had turned and were looking at me. The women, who surrounded me, now faced me and even behind their veils I knew they gawked. The air was brittle with incomprehension. I was anathema to them. Why? What had I done wrong? When would the Creator take me by the hand? But I wouldn't stop now. I couldn't. This was my voice and I had promised myself that I would use it. I would not fail myself a third time. I sang on to the end of the canticle. The bodies around me were still and solid. The words of my song fell dully on their shawled shoulders, like rocks into mud. I sang into a space devoid of spirit. I felt that if I stopped singing, I, too, would be empty of the quickness we call life. I sang, though my voice weakened and my knees wanted to cave, though I knew it was anger that had robbed this house of spirit so quickly.

When I finished, I tugged at Abraham. I hadn't the strength to pick him up. Somehow someone helped us both, out of the house of prayer, down the steps. The helping hands were firm and purposeful. I imagined them gripping the handle of a broom. I imagined myself being the dust tossed into the hair of the mourners at Mother's funeral. I choked on the dust that was me and coughed, doubled over. I moved blindly, clumsy with the weight of their anger.

Abraham said nothing to me on the way home. It didn't matter. I wouldn't have been able to hear him. I was locked behind a wall of silence that preceded me through the streets. I heard nothing. Not even my own breath. I searched my heart for pride that I had used my voice at last. Or if not pride, at least consolation. Instead I found emptiness.

I mustered all my strength and carried Abraham into the house. I kicked the door closed behind me.

Hannah took one look at my face and ran to me. "What is it, Miriam?"

Already the lights flashed and my hands and feet tingled. I thanked the Creator for the small mercy of this warning. I barely managed to place Abraham on the floor before the fit came.

CHAPTER EIGHT

"I know the words to the fourth canticle." Abraham's right hand opened and closed rapidly. "I know them all. You've sung it a hundred times. I know them all."

This was the first time we'd been alone together since my fit. Hannah was now part of the deceit; we formed a trinity — Hannah, Abraham, and me — a trinity that kept my fits hidden from the rest of the world. Abraham had insisted that Hannah keep the secret. And Hannah had agreed instantly, as though any alternative was nonsensical.

Hannah had rubbed my hands and feet with a mixture of oil and wine. She put cold wet cloths on my forehead and muttered and moaned. She had me chew bitter rue and drink a hot brew of saffron. She said it fought spasms. Hope tinged her fearful voice. I didn't correct her. For had not my morning brew with Abraham, that ritual of the past two years, been the very same attack? Tiny spears against desperation. Finally Hannah went out to gather the drying laundry.

And I expected to talk to Abraham of the things that were so filling my chest it burned. But instead he was talking about knowing the words to the canticle.

"What does it matter?" I said impatiently. "Other things are so much more important."

"I wish I could say I didn't know the words." His right hand went up to his head and buried itself in his sandy-colored hair.

"What do you mean?"

Abraham yanked at his hair. "I should have sung with you." He yanked and thrashed. His mouth screwed up in agony.

"Oh, Abraham." I took his frantic right hand and forced the fingers free of the hair. I held it with both my hands and smoothed the back of it against my cheek. "Don't say silly things."

"I should have joined you." Abraham's voice broke. "I'm not brave, Miriam. I have so little to lose, but what little I have I desperately want to keep." A tear made its way down Abraham's cheek and got lost in his thin beard. "I couldn't face their anger."

"There would have been no purpose in your joining me. And this way they're angry only at me, not you. That's better."

Abraham gave a sad laugh. "They'll be angry at me. I taught you the words." He whispered now. "I taught you to read."

My heart fell. "I thought you said it was not written in the Torah that women cannot read." I shook my head. "Even Father spoke of women that read. I heard him telling you. And you told me yourself that there are women heads of the houses of prayer in other places. You spoke of a woman in Rome. You spoke of a woman in Lower Egypt. You said Daniel told you all about them." My words rushed out. They had to prevail. I was crying. "That's where Daniel is now. Egypt." I squeezed Abraham's hand in entreaty. "Tell me Daniel went to Egypt to study with this woman scholar."

"Daniel went to Egypt to incite the Jews against the Romans."

"What?" I laid Abraham's hand carefully on

his chest and sat back on my heels. The coldness of danger made me move slowly. "Why?"

"It was a terrible harvest, the year he left. I was eleven. I remember talk of famine in Egypt. Then the emperor Tiberius distributed grain to the Greeks in Alexandria. But he gave nothing to the Jews. He wanted them to starve."

"But the Jews were under Tiberius' care."

"That same year he expelled all Jews from Rome. Many were sent to Sardinia to fight in battles without weapons. To be slaughtered. Such was Tiberius' care." Abraham's eyes were limpid. Only his voice showed anger.

"The Romans hate us," I said dully, wishing my words would be proved stupid.

"Not all of them. It is said a woman close to Tiberius, his wife or sister, converted to Judaism."

"And for that our people should be starved?" I put my fingertips to my numb lips. "May the Creator keep Daniel safe."

Abraham looked away. "My uncle never feared breaking unjust laws, even when the price might be his life. But I wouldn't break a law, when the price was only their anger."

"No. It cannot be against the law to teach a woman to read. You told me that. Why do you torment yourself? They cannot be angry at you."

"The laws of Moses and Israel are not the strongest laws, Miriam. We pretend they are. But we break those laws more easily than the unwritten laws, the laws people enforce through shame and isolation. There may be women who head synagogues in other places, but it will not happen in our small village. It will not happen in Magdala." Abraham's head jerked spasmodically. "I have broken so many unwritten laws. They will know it now. They will figure out that I taught you." He threw himself back into the pillows. "I should have sung with you. They will vent their anger on me anyway. So I lost what I valued most in life for no purpose whatsoever."

I leaned over Abraham and gently wiped the tears from his cheeks. His anguish was more biting than my own. "What? What did you lose, Abraham?"

"Your respect."

"Never!" I stood up and paced about the room. It was impossible to stand still. My Abraham feared losing my respect. My perfect man. I imagined him singing beside me in the house of prayer. "Don't talk senseless words, Abraham. I never expected you to sing with me. I wouldn't have wanted you to."

"Of course you wanted me to."

"No. You're tone-deaf."

Abraham wrestled with the pillows till he got himself in a position to look at me. He stared. I stared back. Then he laughed. "You mean it, don't you?"

"Of course I do." And now my feet allowed me to stand in one place. "You sing terribly."

"Miriam, what —"

The door opened, without even a knock, before Abraham could finish speaking. Judith came in and shut it behind her.

"I've heard."

My whole body tightened. "What have you heard, Judith?"

"All of it. How you went to the house of prayer and brought that mess of a creature and then . . . then sang!" Judith shook her head. "What on earth is the matter with you, Miriam?"

I looked at Abraham. He was gazing aimlessly at the wall. He gave no indication of being upset at being called a mess. Maybe he thought of himself as a mess. Maybe no one thought reasonably or sensibly. Maybe the whole world was mad. My head felt heavy. I wanted to be outside in the valley, high in a sycamore tree. I looked back at Judith. "I don't really know," I said honestly.

"Well, stop it." Judith spoke with the assertiveness I'd seen her display at the well so often. The assertiveness she showed toward younger women. "Stop all this foolishness. You'll never get a husband, the way you're acting." She thrust her chin toward Abraham. "You mustn't be seen with him anymore."

"Abraham's his name."

Judith peered at me as though I'd said something shocking. "Abraham. You call him by his name? He can't possibly know his name." She stood silent for a moment. Then she spoke slowly, thoughtfully. "Does your father call him Abraham, too?"

"It's his name."

"Yes." She put both hands to her cheeks. She looked chagrined. "Yes, of course. It's the proper thing to do." She shook her head, then dropped her hands. "You are a good girl, Miriam. You have a kind heart. But . . ." She searched for words. "But there are right and wrong ways to show charity."

"Charity?"

"Charity toward this Abraham."

Anger quickened my tongue. "Abraham's my friend."

Judith's face went expressionless. "What could that mean? What kind of friendship could you have with such . . . a one as he?"

"A friendship like any other. Or no, better. Truer."

"But what can you do together, Miriam?"

"We talk. We tell each other things."

Judith stepped forward and took my hand. It was all I could do to keep from pulling it away. "Miriam," she said in a broken voice. Her face was full of pain. Who was she sad for? Surely not for Abraham, though I knew her words echoed in his head. She didn't realize she tortured him.

Judith paused, one hand on her throat. "I thought your father made a mistake not to marry me when you were nine, when I'd been widowed for a year. I thought you needed a mother. And I so wanted a husband. I sometimes think I cannot bear another day living in the home of my mother-in-law. But I have nowhere else to go." She turned my hand over and studied it. "Your father and I have that in common. We have no living parents, no brothers or sisters." Judith now drew slow circles on the palm of my hand with her finger. "But your father said you were the woman of this house, and would be till you married." She gave a sad laugh. "He thought you couldn't bear a replacement for your mother. And so I've waited. Not patiently. No one could accuse me of being patient. But I've waited quietly. I believe I've grown more and more bitter from swallowing bile every day since my husband died." Her finger now traced the veins on the back of my hand. "I made a mistake, Miriam. A mistake for me, surely. But a mistake for you, as well. You needed a mother. Even if only for a few years. I could have been a mother to you. You've been lonely." Her eyes met mine and they brimmed with tears. "I'm so sorry, Miriam."

Sorry? Judith was sorry for me? My anger left as swiftly as it had come. "You don't understand, Judith. I like the way we live. I love Abraham.

I'm not lonely at all. I want to live with Abraham forever."

Judith closed her mouth. I watched the crest of her throat move as she prepared to speak, then stopped herself. Her face was slack, but her eyes were worried. Finally, she whispered, "He . . . Abraham . . . is not the right match for you, Miriam."

The right match for me? I was stunned. Prickles ran down my temples, across my breasts, down my arms. My heart sped. I kept my face impassive, but I was struggling to keep conscious. It was as though in an instant the air had become thick as cream. "Tell me why not, Judith."

Judith brushed away the hair from my forehead. She tilted her own head and looked at me with tenderness. This woman whom I had kept at bay for years was now tender toward me. The world was shifting again. Ever changing.

Judith's fingers moved soft and warm; her palm on my cheek was summer honey. "Miriam, I've been angry at you sometimes. I didn't understand why you ran off alone. I knew you did it. You thought no one noticed, but I did. I didn't understand when I heard you were appearing all over town with Abraham in a cart. I thought you were acting strange on purpose. To draw attention. I thought you were spoiled." She sat and patted the floor beside her. "Please sit."

I sat, keeping my eyes on Judith's face — a face I'd always thought of as sharp. A face I hardly recognized now.

She looked at me for a long moment, her eyes searching. "They told me you knew the words to the song. They said you sang it perfectly."

"Thank you."

Judith gave a short laugh. "Oh, Miriam. It's not praise. They were astonished. I'm astonished. Those songs are for the men to sing. You didn't learn them in the synagogue. Who taught you the words?"

I shook my head. I wouldn't expose Abraham. My dearest Abraham. The man Judith had spoken of as not the right match, and in so doing had transformed him before my very eyes. Abraham had decided to remain hidden in his body. It was not my right to undo what he had done.

"It's all right. I know it was your father. He's unusual, too. That's part of his charm. But I didn't realize before how unusual." Judith looked around the room.

I thought of telling her it wasn't Father who taught me the songs. But if I did, she'd ask the question again, and I couldn't answer it.

Was I interfering in Judith's relationship with Father by not correcting her? For now I knew that Hannah had spoken the truth: Father had vowed to marry this woman whenever I should finally leave his house. He loved Judith. He had to. He'd never marry for less than love. Or was I confusing everything again? It was Mother who had spoken so fervently of love, not Father. Perhaps Father was tired of sleeping alone on cold nights. Perhaps he wanted a companion for his old age, a companion who would hover about him in a way I never had.

I had made Father lonely. And Judith, too. And here she was thinking I was the lonely one — when I wasn't lonely at all. I had Abraham. I looked at the lines by Judith's eyes and thought of the silver strands that had crept into Father's hair while he waited for her.

Judith finished her inspection of our common room and looked back at me. "It seems an ordinary home. But the people in it are extraordinary. I'm going to ask you a question I would never think to ask a woman normally. But I feel I don't know much about you. I made all the wrong assumptions. Tell me, Miriam, do you want to have children?"

I closed my eyes and looked into my heart. Oh, yes. I wanted to hold my babies and roll with them in the grasses of the valley. I wanted to carry them on one hip. I wanted to adorn my daughter with a wide purple cloth belt. And when we walked together in the valley, she could stuff that belt with treasures — the shells of hatched turtle doves, the seeds of the cumin plant. I wanted to bring my son to the hazzan, so he could sit on the ground near the master and repeat his lessons and learn the scripture tales of history and geography. School was a new institution in Magdala. Father had not gone to one, instead learning from his father as his father had learned in turn from his. But times were changing and boys learned together these days. I wanted to see my son with those scholarly boys. And maybe I would talk with the hazzan. Maybe

I would convince this fine man of the house of prayer to give lessons to my daughter, as well.

And I realized I was rocking forward and backward, my breathing labored, rocking with a frenzied mind. Alas, what horrible trick had Judith's question played with that mind? I must banish all thoughts of children. That daughter, that son. I opened my eyes and looked at Judith in my misery.

"Your eyes speak." Judith took a deep breath. "Miriam, I don't even know if you could have children with Abraham. The very idea disgusts me, though I'm trying to think about it now for your sake. But, Miriam, if you did manage to bear a child to Abraham, what would that child be like?"

She said the words. If I were the Lord of Israel, those were the words I would have made her say. The words I hadn't even allowed myself to think. It seemed Judith was always one step ahead of me, her mind prowling where mine didn't dare to go. Oh blessed words: a child with Abraham. Could we? Could Abraham and I join like any other man and woman? And I must follow Judith's questions. I could prowl, too. "Hannah has a strong body. Who knows what child could come from Abraham's seed?"

"But his mind, Miriam. Think of his mind. What would you do with an idiot child?"

Abraham's mind. Abraham's mind was what made me love him. Judith called him an idiot. Jacob did, too. And Jacob's carpenter helpers. And who else? It was just as Abraham had once told me: They all thought he was an idiot. Only Hannah and Father and I knew the truth. Abraham's fear in the house of prayer had been misplaced. Judith hadn't even considered the possibility that Abraham might have been the one to teach me the words of the canticles. No one could ever be angry at Abraham. It was ironic, for no one should ever have been angry at Abraham, but not because he was an idiot — because he was as decent as humans could be. And I found myself speaking words I'd never thought before, words I couldn't deny. "I would never marry another."

"You are of age, Miriam. No one can stop you.

But I do not believe your father would approve of such a match. And I'm sure it is unthinkable to Hannah."

I wouldn't want to displease Father, it was true. And I cared too much for Hannah to disregard her feelings. But as I sat there, it wasn't Father's or Hannah's desires I thought of. It was the desires of the man in the pillows behind me. I wished I knew what Abraham was thinking. I wished he'd speak up.

I waited. I silently begged that man to declare himself. I had proclaimed my love for him. Did he return that love? Oh, I knew Abraham loved me. But did he love me as a man loves a woman? I remembered the mandrake root so long ago and how he'd held it all day, his grip tight and unrelenting, as though around a woman's thigh. And the words of the seventh canticle spoke in my ear:

> The mandrakes give a smell, and at our gates are all manner of pleasant fruits, new and old, which I have laid up for thee, O my beloved.

Yes, Abraham wanted a woman. Would he have me? Would my beloved let us enjoy all manner of pleasant fruits? I prayed for Abraham's words.

But Abraham said nothing.

I flushed with pain. Finally, I spoke. "I will never marry."

Judith nodded. She looked down at her hands and sat quietly for a few minutes. Then she fixed me with her eyes. "Miriam, I have a plan. Let me marry your father. Let me come live with you here. I will treat your friendship with Abraham respectfully. But I will also try to help you change your ways. I will teach you how to be a proper Jewish woman."

Judith's words seemed so simple. Would that Judith could do what she promised. "What would you teach me, Judith?"

"For one, I would teach you to sing in your heart, Miriam. You're not the first woman with a song inside her. But you must keep it from flying out of your mouth. Instead, you must learn to let it fly from your feet."

"You're talking riddles, Judith."

"When Moses parted the Red Sea, he led the

people in song and his sister Miriam led the people in dance. The women danced, too. All the women. From that moment on, our gift — women's gift — was to live the music through our feet. That Miriam is your namesake. 'Miriam' means 'beloved of the Lord Himself.' You are beloved, Miriam. Listen to the lesson of the scriptures; it's as though they were written for you. You used to dance, sweet Miriam. When you were little, I watched you dance on your way to the well with Hannah." Judith smiled. "Even my husband Saul noticed. You were graceful. The swirls of your crimson shift caught the eye. I had always wanted sons. But you made me wish I'd be blessed with daughters, as well." Judith was quiet for a moment. "At some point you stopped dancing. I don't know exactly when, but I know you haven't danced for years. I can teach you dances, Miriam. I will take you by the hand."

Her words were balm, soothing and warm. I was too old to have a mother, yet sudden longing filled me. Judith had told me the true meaning of my own name, and in doing so she had named me anew, given me a second beginning. "I'd like to dance again. I'd like to be a proper woman like you."

Judith laughed. "I didn't say like me. I hope you won't be like me, Miriam. The Creator didn't see fit to bless me with female children as well as males. He didn't see fit to bless me with children at all. That's why my mother-in-law hates me. If Saul hadn't died, she would have pressed him to divorce me. As it was, she had already suggested a second wife for him. But his death came and stopped all plans." Judith leaned toward me with a rueful smile. "I suppose I'm as much a misfit as you. Just in different ways. No sensible man would marry a barren woman. But your father doesn't let sense rule his life. He told me he could never bear to risk losing another wife in childbirth anyway." Judith rubbed her legs. "Oh, Miriam, I don't care if you do all sorts of improper things within the house. I will do my best to be a good friend to you. And if you let me, I will be a mother of sorts, though we may both be too old to follow ordinary patterns there. Still, we can make new patterns." Judith stopped rubbing and spoke with firmness. "But when you are outside the house, you must limit yourself. You must not stray too far from the customs." Her face went solemn. "For your own good."

Customs. The unwritten laws. Judith was as much afraid of them as Abraham was. Abraham's fear had silenced him. Had Judith's fear made her seem so bossy all these years? "And what about Abraham?"

"What about him?"

"What would you do with him?"

"Hannah and he could stay on, just as they have in the past."

"And could I go places with him?"

"Not through the town, Miriam. Please. But you could go to the valley if you like. The valley is safe, I think."

I wanted to say yes. If it had been up to me alone, I'd have agreed right then and there. "I have to talk with Abraham about it first."

Judith sucked in her bottom lip. "Miriam, he can't understand you. I know you wish he could. I know your wish makes you imagine things. Like a child with a doll." She shook her head. "Abraham's not a doll, Miriam."

My face went hot. I took Judith by the arm and pulled her over to Abraham's pillows. I looked from one to the other. "Talk to each other. Please."

Abraham stared through me.

I couldn't bear it. This was no moment to hide. "Talk!"

Judith cleared her throat. "Hello, Abraham."

Abraham didn't even blink.

Judith waited. Then she pulled me to her and closed me in her arms like a small girl, though I stood a head taller than her. My breath floated lightly above her shoulder. "Let him be. He has so little peace as it is. Please, Miriam. Sweet Miriam. Let him be."

CHAPTER NINE

"You could at least have talked to her."

"It's better that she thinks I'm an idiot."

"You always say things are better your way!" I got on my knees and faced Abraham head-on. I wanted to cry to him the sorrow in my heart. For he was my friend, a comfort to me. I wanted to rail and rave at him. For he was my enemy, the origin of my pain. But I hadn't the courage to do either. I spoke only the mentionable. "You always want secrets. I'm so sick of secrets I could scream. Judith is good. We can trust her. I'm going to tell her everything."

"Do you know what they'd think — how they'd feel — if they knew I was locked inside this body?" Abraham's voice was full of foreboding.

"If they knew you were in there, they'd talk to

you. It's like Father said to Jacob — some of us are fortunate and others of us aren't. They know that in their hearts. If you would only talk to them, they'd realize you were just like them."

"That's exactly it, Miriam. As long as I'm an idiot, they can bear to have me around. They can tell themselves they are generous of heart and ignore me. But if they know I can see things and understand them, if they know I'm like them inside, it's too much. It's too horrible. They fear it could happen to them. Who I am, Miriam, who you are — what has happened to us, it could happen to anyone." Abraham's voice caught. "They won't allow themselves to think that way. They'll find a reason, for random misfortune terrifies. If they know I'm in here, they'll say I'm evil. They'll say it's not me who speaks, but the evil within. They'll fear even more that whatever has possession of my body can leap out and take possession of theirs. My only hope is that they do not see me as a person. Then they will not need to banish me."

I shook my head. "You can't be right. If you spoke to them as you speak to me, they would hear. People can't be so stupid."

"You were stupid, Miriam. You thought your fits came from demons. You've had three fits now. That would mean three demons live inside you. But you know in your heart you are pure."

My chest went cold. Did I know in my heart I was pure? I was not even being honest with Abraham now. I was hiding my feelings, pretending I'd never declared my love for him. Was that pure? But this was not a moment to argue the point. I knew in my heart that Abraham was pure. I knew that as well as I knew the Creator was pure. "You taught me who you are, Abraham. You can teach them."

"They won't learn."

"How can you say that! How can you know?"

"Because I saw it happen."

"What?" I shook my head in confusion. "What did you see?"

Abraham hesitated. "I was in Safed. I was very young." He spoke slowly, as though each word took effort. "I saw a man with diseased limbs. He could walk. He begged. And he had a bowl for alms." Abraham let himself roll onto his back. He looked at the ceiling. "A young boy ran by and scooped from the bowl. The beggar stumbled after him. He caught the boy by the arm and scolded him, shaking him roughly. A crowd gathered. Not many people, maybe six or seven. But they gathered quickly. They told him not to touch the boy. They told him not to touch anyone. They told him to leave. And he argued. He pleaded his case. He'd been robbed. It was clear who was in the right and who was in the wrong. One by one they left. I thought he had convinced them. I was close to a wall, with Daniel. I wanted to go talk to the beggar, to congratulate him. I asked Daniel to carry me over close to him. But the people came back. Their hands were full. They threw stones at him." Abraham closed his eyes. He shivered. When he opened them again, he spoke quietly. I had to strain to listen. "Daniel shouted, and soon other men shouted. They stopped the crowd. But do you know how they stopped them?"

I shook my head wordlessly, though Abraham wasn't looking at me — he couldn't see my shaking head.

"They said that the Romans would get involved if there was a death. They said stoning was a judicial sentence and no one could do it without the court's approval. So the people dropped their stones out of fear. That's the only reason."

My breath filled my hands, which covered my face. I waited for the rush of blood to slow. After many minutes, I could speak again. "Abraham, the people who stopped the stoning were decent. And the decent people prevailed."

Abraham twisted until he faced me. "And if they hadn't been there?"

"Decent people will always be there."

"You speak nonsense, Miriam."

I couldn't imagine the people of Magdala with stones in their hands. I couldn't imagine the people of Israel anywhere with stones in their hands. But maybe that was because I refused to. I looked into Abraham's sea eyes. The Sea of Galilee was also called the Lake of Kinneret because it was harp-shaped, like the kinneret that my mother used to play. Abraham's eyes didn't move; the Sea was still today. "I will never tell people about you, Abraham. I will never betray you."

And so it passed that Judith and Father married and I danced with the women at their wedding feast and Judith came to live with us. I didn't speak again of marrying Abraham, nor did I ever speak of Abraham's true self.

I often wondered if Abraham thought about my conversation with Judith that day. We never spoke of it. Abraham never acknowledged that I had told Judith in his presence that I loved him. Yet we seemed to be more careful in how we touched each other after that. When I'd pull him into the cart, I'd lift him from behind and hold him far enough from my body that my breasts wouldn't press against his back. Whenever his right hand reached for me, it was my hand he touched, never higher up on my arm, or my face, or my hair. We hadn't been so physically distant before that. Before that our bodies had been facts no more compelling than the fact of stones and trees and dirt. They had a size and shape and texture that simply were. Now our bodies were ideas. They could enter the mind and fill every crevice. They were to be avoided.

Our talk seemed more guarded, too. We read the Torah together now, whenever we had the privacy we needed. I could have counted on my fingers and toes the number of times up till then that I had touched the sacred scrolls that made up the books of the Torah. Now suddenly I was touching them almost daily. Exhilaration made me dizzy the first time I carried one across the room and unrolled it beside Abraham.

Abraham delighted in discussing with me the great women leaders of Israel. But now he didn't talk of Daniel and the women Daniel had spoken of who lived in our times. We turned, instead, to a higher authority — to the scriptures. We told each other the ancient stories of Deborah, the judge and leader, who commanded the people in battles with the Philistines. We spoke of how Barak, the man leader, turned to Deborah for guidance. We reveled in Jael's pounding a nail though the soft temples of King Sisera's head as the Philistines slept, and thus saving her people. And Abraham loved most reading with me the tales of Miriam, my namesake, who was called a prophet.

A woman prophet. A woman with a voice that would be heard. A woman who sang a war victory song. Would that I could take a timbrel in my hand and place a crown of olive wreaths on my head and celebrate victory over the battles of my life, as Miriam had done.

Abraham and I spoke of other things, too. We spoke of my vegetable and herb garden. We spoke of birds and trees. We spoke of the people of the village. But we never spoke about each other anymore. We never spoke our fears. Nor our hopes.

Maybe Abraham had no hopes. I wasn't sure I did.

I missed Abraham, though I was with him in the same house day after day. In my dreams we were close again. In my dreams we climbed the hills that surrounded the Sea of Galilee. We followed the River Jordan south. We sat among the flowering mustards that grew as tall as trees. And nothing, nothing kept us apart. But when I'd awaken, we'd keep our respectful distance once again.

Sometimes I didn't want to wake. Sometimes the distance of Abraham during the day left me lost and disoriented. At those times I'd study the Torah most intensely. I wanted help in this passage through life.

Judith was true to her word. She taught me new and intricate dances. My eager feet couldn't learn fast enough. They demanded more, and Judith taught more. But she watched my face closely. She said my mouth moved in silent song. She played a reed flute and three months after her wedding to Father she bought me one, saying I needed to make music with my mouth. I remembered sitting beside Mother as she played the harp. Father had given that harp to one of her sisters when she died. My hands had itched with the desire for those strings as I watched them carted away.

The flute didn't have the same attraction. Flutes to me meant Mother's funeral. So my hands, which had been so greedy for the harp, were now reluctant on the flute. My fingers touched the holes gingerly. Yet the notes that came forth were not mournful. They rose light and gay, and soon I came to trust them and my fingers moved more quickly and my lungs were happy to swell.

Judith and I filled the house with birdlike melodies. Then we danced again. We laughed together and wove, side by side with Hannah,

mindful that woolwork kept a woman virtuous.
We spun yarn at night under the moonlight. Judith told stories of our people's history as we worked, stories her mother had told to her. And every time the Israelites triumphed over an oppressor, we laughed. Judith came home from the well and told stories of the village children's antics that morning. And we laughed again. We laughed often. But my laughter was never wholly carefree. I think hers was not, either.

Yet we shared a kind of happiness that was new to me. I had helped Hannah all my life, so the details of household work were known to me. But I had never valued them highly. Now I learned to lose myself in grinding corn. I discovered the spirituality in being diligent, in creating a home in which faith could find firm footing. I saw the devotion in Hannah's eyes as she washed her hands or cleaned the dishes, following rituals that our people had kept for so many generations. I saw the glow of purity on Judith's cheeks when she came home from the mikvah, like a new bride. I thought of all the women of Israel everywhere renewing themselves monthly, offering themselves as pure gifts to their husbands, ever optimistic, ever generous. Women formed the filament of continuity, and my soul spun itself out on that holy thread.

For the first time since my fits had begun, I could pay attention to the world around me as a member, not just an observer. I saw Hannah move with respect in Judith's presence. I listened to their careful words, one to another, and rejoiced when they finally talked freely without guarding themselves. Gradually, gradually I saw Hannah relax in the realization that she was still secure, that Judith accepted her and Abraham without question.

I saw Father step more quickly, his eyes shine more brightly. I noticed for the first time how large his hands were as they reached for Judith inside our home. I saw the color come to her cheeks and her lips part as she looked at him. I was careful to go to bed early on those nights. And if sleep did not come swiftly, I plugged my ears with my fingers and allowed Father and Judith their private world.

These were the people I belonged to, and we were growing together as a family.

The only one who did not seem to change with

Judith's coming was Abraham. He began by being silent in her presence and he persisted in that. She began by watching him. Then by doing her weaving near him. Then, finally, by addressing him. More than once I came into the house with dirt under my nails from working the garden to find Judith sitting beside Abraham playing her flute or recounting some event of the day before. Abraham's eyes wandered, never lighting on her, never acknowledging that her attention was directed at him. More than once Judith blew in from the outdoors like a wild wind and found Abraham propped against the wall, a scroll on the floor before him. She walked over and unrolled the scroll just a bit more, murmuring a word or two about the strength one gained from the holy scriptures.

Abraham didn't look at her. He stopped reading. He glanced vaguely at the flowing script, then away, as though the words on the page were meaningless — as though Judith's murmurs were undifferentiated from the sigh of the wind.

Judith didn't talk to me of Abraham so I never knew for sure, but I believed she realized he was inside that body, I believed Abraham fooled no one. Judith spoke of him and to him with respect. And if she did it only for my benefit, she never let me know that.

But Abraham didn't relent. Sometimes I wondered if he was punishing me, if he refused to let Judith into his life because she had so cleanly come into mine. I tried to ask him once, but I couldn't say what I needed to say in order to get him to answer honestly. How could I ask Abraham if he missed me, if he was jealous for my care, without opening up the issue we had both tacitly agreed to ignore?

Still, despite my newfound friendship with Judith, I didn't give up my visits to the valley with Abraham. I couldn't. Being with Abraham, even in our now limited way, was my lifeline. We read or talked in the valley. I didn't climb the sycamores and sing anymore. The flute sang for me without the pain of words. But still I had to be outdoors, in the open. And I had to be alone with Abraham. Even if being alone with Abraham gave me the loneliest moments of my life.

Things defined themselves in contradictory

ways. Judith was ours now — an addition. Yet I, who had not been lonely before, was now terribly lonely in my womanhood. I shared with Judith and Hannah an aspect of femininity that gave dignity to my day. But I was aware of another aspect of femininity that suffered from lack of satisfaction, satisfaction only one man could provide.

No unwanted offers of marriage came, though I no longer went about the village in a way unseemly to a proper woman. I didn't know whether that was because Judith fended off matches, as she had promised to do, or whether no offers were extended. I suspected the latter. Certainly I was as beautiful a woman as any in our village, though I was taller than half the men. I felt the eyes of lust on me even as I walked to the mikvah once a month. But it was only lust, not admiration. My behavior was too strange, even if I didn't wander, even if I kept silent in the house of prayer these days.

And I did go to the house of prayer. Judith took me with her often. It seemed to please Father. He always said an approving word when we came home. The passing of time smoothed away the worry that had come to Father's brow after my singing in the house of prayer that one time. The passing of time dulled the edge of that knife I had known since I realized my love for Abraham. I came to believe that the passing of time saw the death of all things, good and bad. I came to think of passions as vanities, illusive and transitory.

Time passed slowly. Toward the end of the bitter winds and cloudy weather the year I was sixteen, Abraham got sick. It was a colder year than most. We had gone out well bundled up, but a storm came and we were soaked by the time we got home. I spread our clothes before the fire and insisted on rubbing Abraham dry myself, though Hannah was mortified at my seeing his nakedness. She forbade me from tending to him, when she had never forbade me from anything before. But I ignored her, just as I ignored Judith.

I unwrapped Abraham as a woman would unwrap a child. It was easy to think of his body as a child's, for his limbs were as thin as a boy's and he had no power to object. Or, at least, he did not exercise that power. I exercised power — power over myself. I would not think of Abraham as a man. I tended to him as a servant does. I did what I had to do. It was my job.

For I blamed myself for Abraham's fever. I knew the skies from my many days in the valley. I should have read their message. I should have tasted their moisture. But restlessness seized me. I needed to walk about and suck the clean cold air into my lungs. So I had taken Abraham out without the proper precautions. And now he shivered in my arms and his thin chest radiated unnatural heat.

The fever lasted three days before it broke. And even after that it kept coming back. Never so severely as at first, but still high, followed by racking chills. Abraham's skin grew taut, until the ribs of his chest could be counted with the eye. He coughed often, a deep wet cough from the center of his being. His eyes varied from shiny wet to listless dull. Even his hair lost its luster. I stayed at his side and anointed his head and feet with oils I had scented with the sweet calamus.

I couldn't tell him the scripture stories, for he knew them all much better than I. So I made up stories to fend off boredom. I took him on boats through crocodile waters. We fed carob pods to hippopotamuses. We threw mimosa flowers into the air and storks caught them and flew away, leaving rainbow streaks in the sky.

I wouldn't leave his side.

The first night Hannah appealed to Father. She kneeled at his feet. "It isn't right. Please. Tell Miriam she cannot stay by his side through the night." Her plea shocked us all. Hannah had never dared suggest action to Father before. She had never dared point out right and wrong to the man of the house.

Judith stood beside Hannah and wrung her hands. I waited to see if she, too, would join forces against me. My fists closed until my nails bit into my palms. I had to stay by Abraham. It was essential. I prepared for battle with a rising sense of desperation.

But Judith held her tongue. Oh kind Judith, oh true friend. She stayed silent against her better judgment. Her silence was fair and just — whether she knew this or not, I now did. For Hannah's words had brought me new realization.

It was not wrong for me to stay by Abraham's side through the night. No. I was not tending to Abraham as a servant, after all; I was tending to him as a woman to a man she loved. And it mattered not that the love was unrequited. I had fooled myself these past three years, the years since my last fit — the years since Judith had come to live with us. My passion for Abraham burned as hot as his fever. It had never stopped burning.

Father remained silent for a long moment.

Too long. Hannah's voice rose, betraying her internal battle against breaking into a wail. "If you allow this, it is your doing, not mine." Fear scrabbled in her throat. "Not Abraham's." She doubled over in paroxysms of coughing.

Hannah still walked the edge, always fearful of falling off. She feared Father casting her out as much as I feared Abraham rebuking me. I took Abraham's hot hands in mind and held them tight.

Father reached for Hannah's hands at the same moment. He pulled her to her feet. "It is my doing." He turned and looked at me with misery in his eyes. I knew then that he understood. My wonderful, unlikely father. He had always understood, even when he proclaimed he didn't, even when he wished he didn't. He comforted Hannah and Judith now, but all he could do for me was let me be.

Those three nights I crooned to Abraham in his restless sleep. Only when the fever finally passed did I retreat to my own bed mat. But whenever the fever returned, I took up my station by his side.

Whether the illness broke Abraham's spirit or the illness brought him to his senses, I didn't know — but the illness surely changed Abraham. For now he spoke to me and Hannah and Father in front of Judith. And when she played her flute for him, he thanked her.

In full spring, Abraham's cough ended and one day he begged me to take him to the valley to see the lilies. Hannah was against the idea, but Judith took my side. Abraham had to have the pleasure of the lilies this year. He deserved it.

The valley was muddy that day, but the winds were warm already. "It is a perfect day, Abraham," I found myself saying over and over, "a perfect day." I was so happy to be out of the house finally, I could almost have sung my pleasure.

"Miriam, let's stop here."

"In the middle of the mud?"

"I'm tired. Do you care if you get muddy?"

I smiled and lifted Abraham down to the ground. His body was so light, I thought of a child again — light as it had been the very first time I'd lifted him. I marveled at the deception of our bodies.

I sat beside him, comfortable and easy. Not a worry crossed my mind. The fit took me totally by surprise. As the air around me flashed bright, I thought if only I could grab myself and pin myself down, I could keep it from happening. I screamed silently inside my head. I deafened myself.

The next thing I felt was Abraham's right hand, stroking my hair in jerky moves. My head rested on his left arm and we lay side by side in the mud. I looked at his face. He was looking off in the distance. Then he caught my eye and smiled.

Abraham had the sweetest smile of anyone I ever knew. His teeth were white, for Hannah rubbed them with salt every day, just as she did her own. There was mud in his beard. I thought of what a struggle it must have been for him in his weakened state to get to me and maneuver me onto his arm like this. I took his right hand and inspected it.

Abraham laughed. "No teeth marks. Your fourth demon seems milder than the earlier ones. Your mouth didn't foam."

His laugh was open and genuine. His laugh was everything good in the world. And before I knew what I would do, I was kissing his mouth, and he was kissing mine. The fierce purity of our passions knotted us together on the Creator's earth. And I discovered, oh thanks be to everything holy, that all my doubts and fears were ungrounded, for Abraham had no trouble loving me.

We went home hours later covered with mud. Hannah and Judith met us and I saw the question in Judith's eyes. I looked at her and wanted to shout with joy. Instead, I smiled. She hesitated, visibly struggling with her own confusion and fears. Then she smiled back. Hannah saw our exchange. But she didn't join in the smiling. I kissed her cheek.

The three of us washed clothes that day, while Abraham slept in the pillows. From our rooftop I imagined I could hear the waterfalls on the northern part of the River Jordan. I showered in those cascades, washed new before the Creator by the rush of water over stone. I stepped into the silent spring air, clean and ready.

The fever returned that night. This time it came and stayed. Some days it would be mild, only Abraham's forehead would be warm. But on other days his hands were hot, and on the worst days even his feet were hot. I took over his full care from Hannah then. She didn't argue with me. For now Judith and Father had aligned themselves with me. Consummation made as valid a marriage by Talmudic Law as any contract or exchange of goods. And Father couldn't begrudge the fact that Abraham and I had not asked for his blessing — for it was obvious that a situation such as ours rendered foolish that formality.

I was the one to bathe Abraham and feed him

now. He seemed to grow smaller before my eyes. His body curled. His eyes, that cool blue, now burned from deep hollows. Yet he smiled at me often. At night we slept side by side and he whispered the canticles in my ear. And, yes, his cheeks were as a bed of spices, as sweet flowers. And, yes, his mouth was most sweet, yea, he was altogether lovely.

I am my beloved's, and my beloved is mine: he feedeth among the lilies.

And even on the nights when fever ruled him, we were lovers in the dark. Those nights were like precious jewels, each one glittering with a perfect brilliance.

Two weeks passed and Abraham faded day by day. I knew he was dying. We all knew, though we didn't speak of it. Our lovemaking now was kisses on palms, breath on cheeks.

One night before Abraham slept, he insisted I dance for him. Father and Judith and Hannah slept. The moon was rich and moonlight flooded in from the window, lighting more brightly than our oil lamp alone ever could. I held my arms out to both sides and swirled around Abraham again and again.

"You are like a *magdal*," he said. "You are tall like the tower our town Magdala was named after. My beautiful Miriam."

I smiled and lay down beside the man I cherished.

"With your arms out like that, it was as though you flew. As though you were an angel." Abraham took my hand. "Miriam, can I choose the name?"

I pressed his hand to my cheek. I kissed the pulse of his wrist. Of course he would have realized my blood had not come that month, even though it was only a few days late. Of course he knew my rhythms. Abraham's body might fail him, but his mind never would. His heart never would.

"Tell me," I whispered. Would our child be named Elon, after the oak, or Tamar, after the palm tree? Or would we have Rachel, a ewe, or Akbor, a mouse? I thought of the doves in the terebinth that shaded Mother's grave. Would we have Yona, a dove? Or maybe Zeitan, an olive, for Father and his generous olive grove? I tensed with anticipation.

"Isaac."

A biblical name. Of course. It was the name the Abraham of the scriptures had given to his son, the Abraham whose obedience to the Creator had been so tested. *Isaac* meant "laughter." Yes, my Abraham had chosen well. We would have a son, of course. A child Abraham would never see. My son and my husband were losing each other. They would never share laughter. The pain was savage.

I kissed Abraham on the mouth and his breath filled me. It was his final breath.

In the morning Hannah and I prepared his body for burial. Those who touch the dead are unclean, yet that uncleanliness is good, for they say it comes from charity. I knew this was true now. I anointed Abraham's head and feet. I washed his body tenderly. But I did not do these duties out of love. I did them out of charity. The body that we buried was not Abraham. It was meaningless flesh and blood. Abraham was the spirit that had given my life direction and form since I was ten years old. Abraham was the father of the child within me. Abraham had given me his last breath and I would carry it inside for the rest of my life.

CHAPTER TEN

Though I was tall, I was not, in fact, a *magdal* — a tower. I was thin. And my thinness meant that my rounded belly showed early, even at the start of summer. I wore loose black shifts, but eyes settled on my belly when I went to the well. Those eyes knew.

Father knew, too. At first he looked at me with incredulity, then a sadness settled on him. He spoke to me of Abraham only once, the day the letter returned. Hannah blanched the instant she saw it. Father explained that he had sent word to Daniel of Abraham's death. But the letter returned unopened. Hannah put her face in her hands and sobbed. I fed the letter to the fire and hugged Hannah from behind, resting my cheek between her shoulders blades, crooning, crooning.

The silence that had swallowed Abraham now swallowed Daniel, as well. And Father would have it swallow Isaac, for he never spoke to me of the baby within me. I knew he thought about the blessing of a public marriage. I knew he wished that Abraham had placed the ring on my finger and spoken the words, "I take you as my wife according to the Laws of Moses and Israel." Father would have served as witness, and surely some neighbor man would have served as well. We could have been married before the eyes of the village. That's what Father regretted — that the village hadn't been forced to recognize the legitimacy of our union. I heard him say those very words to Judith. Perhaps he knew that lack would be dangerous. Perhaps he had forebodings.

We would have had a public marriage, Abraham and I, for Isaac's sake, so that our son would be called the son of Abraham, instead of the son of Miriam, like some bastard. But Abraham had died before I'd even had the confidence to truly believe Isaac lived within me.

But, really, I didn't care how Isaac would be called. He'd be Father's heir. He'd have a secure place in Magdala, no matter what. And I didn't care what the villagers would think of me. I fully believed that their opinions didn't matter. All that mattered was that Abraham and I had the Creator's blessing on our union. Of that I was sure. For no baby was conceived out of greater love than Isaac.

I think Father eventually came round to this position, as well. He gradually lost his edginess. He almost smiled as he watched me engrossed in some homekeeping task, for I helped in most of the chores these days. Once my thirty days of mourning were past, I shed the sackcloth and donned black, and even before that I went to work energetically.

For without Abraham to tend to, my hands felt empty. Brutally empty. At first I reached for the shadows as though for my beloved. Every whisper of the wind seemed his voice. Every waft of flower perfume seemed his breath. My senses were assailed with memories of Abraham. But I knew a sad mother makes a lost child. So for Isaac's sake, I calmed my heart. I was steadfastly dry-eyed. And I didn't allow my hands to clutch at the shadows. I wouldn't allow them to be empty. Oh, no. I filled them with tasks. I worked hard in the house. But I also took every opportunity to go outdoors. I insisted on fetching the water several times a day.

Judith often went with me to the well. And sometimes we took walks together in the valley. She asked me to show her where I used to go with Abraham and she looked at everything with wide, absorbing eyes. She held my arm as we walked and she'd tell me over and over again those tales her mother had told her about our people's past tribulations. I knew the stories by heart now and yet I never tired of hearing Judith tell them in her mellow voice that paused at just the right moments.

She joined me now in tending the kitchen garden and she spent hours hunting one day for a wild cumin plant that she carried home carefully and transplanted into the center of our garden. I knew that she already planned how she would assemble the oil, wine, and cumin for the plaster that would go upon the wound left by circumcision. I listened to her hum as we worked the earth. Then we sat in the summer sun side by side.

Toward the end of my fifth month of pregnancy, as Judith and I were sitting in the grasses, she put her hand on my belly. She'd done that a lot lately. "Have you felt him yet?"

I smiled, happy to yield my secret, my surprise. "It started like a fish. A swirly, ripply fish."

Judith laughed. "How long ago?"

"More than a moon."

She moved her face close to my belly and called out, dulcet and cooing, "Little one, little one, swim hard. Grow strong. The Sea of Galilee is yours. Only swim. Swim for your mother. Swim for your grandmother."

I couldn't hold in the news any longer. "Wait!" I got up and I was running and running around Judith. Around and around.

"Miriam!" She reached for me with both hands. "Miriam, stop!"

"Just wait!" I ran till I could no more. Then I flopped down beside her and pulled up my shift. I took her hand.

"Miriam, you mustn't . . ."

"Hush!" At first all I felt was my blood rushing, rushing. Then he stirred. "Here!" I pressed her hand to my right side. "See? He's awake."

"Oh! Oh, Miriam! I felt him."

"Push!"

Judith looked at me with large eyes.

"Go on, Judith, push as hard as you can."

"Little one," she called, "here I am." Judith pushed. She laughed. "Oh, Miriam. He kicked me!"

"Yes. You pushed him and he pushed right back."

Judith's eyes fixed on my face as the significance of Isaac's actions sank in. "He can kick! He can move his legs!"

"Yes, Judith."

"Oh, Miriam, he can move however he wants."

I laughed Abraham's laugh. "Yes, Judith."

And we hugged and cried and hugged.

Those were warm days, together days. I was hardly ever alone, except when I visited Abraham's grave, which I did daily. It was near a sycamore, the closest sycamore to the terebinth where Mother was buried. I dropped little things in Abraham's cart, which was parked in the shade of the sycamore. The tip of a jasmine branch weighted with blooms. A sparrow feather. A harp-shaped piece of wood. Things we would have passed together if we were still bumping our way through the valley. Things we would have remarked on together.

I talked to the two of them, Mother and Abraham, daily, but briefly. For the life within me spurred me to want living contact. I never failed to ask Father about his day and to listen closely to the details of his business. If Hannah paused in chopping vegetables, I took up the knife and worked with her, shoulder to shoulder. And I relished, especially, every moment with Judith.

It was in the valley that Judith surprised me — she asked me to sing. So there I sat, dressed in mourning, singing the canticles as though the world were nothing but beautiful. I couldn't get Judith to sing with me, but she liked to hear me sing, that much I knew. She couldn't hide her pleasure. She even said once that my son would be born singing. I thought of Abraham and how tone-deaf he was and I laughed. I wanted my son to sing, but, oh, how lovely it would be if he sang off-tune.

Hannah watched me carefully. She fed me more than usual. She combed out my long hair and touched my back every time she passed by. But she rarely smiled. And every day she went to the house of prayer, just as she had done when Abraham was alive. She didn't say it, but I thought she prayed for Isaac. She seemed to step more lightly after Isaac starting kicking within me. Perhaps her fears lessened.

I had no fears. My future was more wonderful than I had dared to hope it could be for the past six years. My past dimmed. My present was a time of preparation among women. We wove baby sleep gowns. We talked of calling in the mohel on the eighth day after birth to perform the circumcision with his flint knife. I dreamed of rubbing my son with salt to harden his skin. He would be a bekor, a first child who is a male, the greatest pleasure. I would nurse him well and when I weaned him, we would have the most elaborate feast, in memory of the biblical Abraham's celebration of the time Sarah stopped suckling her Isaac. We talked of the sacrifice of the lamb and the turtle dove that I would offer forty days after his birth as a burnt sacrifice. We never stopped talking.

I could have had that child, poor sweet boy. He was healthy and would have grown strong and smart. Isaac would have been a fitting name for him. He would have been raised with a ready laugh.

But it didn't turn out like that.

My downfall was an innocent idiot boy. I don't know where he came from. One day I learned that a group of traveling beggars had come to town and among them was the idiot boy. I heard it at the well, where I had come alone, for Hannah and Judith had gotten an early start on milling the barley. Sarah, my friend from early childhood days, spoke of him to her younger sister Susanna, who had recently married. Sarah shifted her baby from her right hip to her left. Her two-year-old sat on the ground and played with pebbles.

"Did you see the boy?" I asked.

Sarah turned her head toward me. A hint of

fear flickered in her eyes. She quickly covered it with a smile. "Miriam, oh, I didn't notice you."

They had all noticed me, of course. I knew I would be the target of their talk once I left the well. But I didn't waste time acknowledging Sarah's lie. "The idiot boy, did you see him?"

"Of course not. He stays in the marketplace."

I wanted to ask if he was crippled. I wanted to hold Sarah by the arm and steady myself as I received her answer. I moved closer. She backed away. For an instant I wanted to beseech — for we had once been close. Instead I said, "How do you know he's an idiot?"

Sarah shrugged. "He must be." She bent over and took her toddler by the hand. "I have to hurry now. Susanna, come along. I need you. Good-bye, Miriam." The four of them left.

I didn't hesitate. Sarah, Susanna, the children — it would not matter if I never saw them again, but I had to see the idiot boy. I knew nothing about him; he was a total stranger. But the very fact that he was called an idiot made him important to me. I took shortcuts through alleys, using our town tower as my guide. I had not walked these routes for three years — the years in which I had lived within the beneficence of Judith's watch. But my feet knew them well. Within a half hour, I arrived. I worked my way though the crowds of the marketplace with determination.

I must have looked very strange, I must have. Later when I struggled to make sense of what happened that day, I tried to see myself through others' eyes. My hair streamed out from under my headcloth in wild ringlets. I wore no veil, since I had intended to go only to the well, to be only among women. My shift was loose and shapeless; it gave no sign that I was a woman of means. Perhaps those who saw me and knew Father thought that he had disowned me, given my dress and behavior. Perhaps some didn't even recognize me as Father's daughter, for I had grown since the last time Abraham and I had wandered the market. Perhaps I looked like a stranger to Israel herself. But I was unaware of how I looked to others. It was the last thing on my mind.

I searched the places where the familiar beggars stayed, the beggars of Magdala. In vain.

Then I heard them, the new beggars. One of them tapped a drumskin. The very unfamiliarity of the sound identified them. I followed the irregular beat.

There were five of them, three women, a man, and one little boy.

They stayed near the wall outside the hall of prostitutes, with bowls for donations set on the ground.

The man sat in the dust and ate from a bunch of grapes that he must have picked from a vineyard on his way to the market — for while it was theft to take grapes off a vendor's pile at the market, beggars had the right to pick fruits from orchards so long as they ate them themselves and carried neither basket nor sickle. No one would die of hunger on farming land.

One of the women sat beside him and gnawed at a crust of bread distractedly, as though her hunger was past but her teeth wouldn't listen.

But I didn't look long at the man or the women. It was the boy I'd come for.

At first I thought the boy was blind. His face was vague, his mouth hung open, drool dangled from his bottom lip. I walked up to him. "Boy? What's your name, boy?"

His face didn't change expression. Perhaps he hadn't realized I was talking to him. I put my hand on his shoulder and leaned over him. "Little boy. Dear little boy, can you tell me your name?"

My words seemed to register now, but they registered very little. If there was an intelligent mind in this child, I saw no evidence of it. He was not a trapped mind yearning for contact. He was not another Abraham. Perhaps that was better, for this child might never know loneliness. He might even be too dull to know yearning. There was nothing I could do for him.

I touched his cheek lightly. He stared through me. One of the women came over and pulled the boy to her. Her breasts swung above a half-starved torso. Her eyes showed no fear, but neither did they show friendliness. Her face was an animated version of his. The boy threw his arms around her hips and clung.

I straightened up and took a step backward. A hissing laugh came from the side. Two men leered at me from across a table piled high with pelts. I quickly lowered my head, my cheeks burning. But I raised it again, just as quickly. A scourge on those men. I would walk home with my head high. This was my town, too. This was my home. How dare the thickskulls of society force these beggars to this wall here? How dare they take away every chance of happiness of the idiot boy? How dare they limit the paths my feet could travel in life? I turned to leave.

A hand grabbed me by the arm and twirled me around, managing to pull me in one swift painful move through the doorway into the hall of prostitutes.

"It's Miriam. I thought so. What has it been, four years now? And still, I'd know you anywhere." Jacob, the carpenter I'd watched with Abraham so many times, the man who had threatened us with a raised arm, pushed his fleshy face up near mine. Wine made his breath heavy; it slurred his speech. "I heard you slept with the idiot man." His eyes moved down to my belly. "I see I heard right."

I pulled free and walked past him to the doorway.

His arm was around my expanding waist in a flash. "Now you came after the new little idiot boy. Is that it?" He pulled me farther into the hall, farther from the doorway. "A seduction?"

I pushed him in the chest and tried to free myself. But his grip grew stronger than I'd have expected for a man going to fat like him, a man so obviously drunk. His face came up to my neck and he kissed me there now, as his free hand moved across my shift and stopped at my breast. "I knew there was something wrong with you. You came seeking to my shop years ago," he said loudly. "Today you came seeking again. And I am a man of charity."

I shouted, "Let me go." I kicked and ripped at his hair. I looked around frantically. But the crowds were outside the hall and if there were people in this hall, they were behind hung curtains.

I screamed.

And screamed.

And screamed.

For the first time, a fit did not take me against my will. As Jacob threw me to the floor, I had two prayers at once. My first was that the Creator should keep me alive. Isaac would be ready to be born in just three more months and I had to stay alive if I was to be the mother he needed. My second prayer was that a fit would come. For Jacob would believe the common fallacy that fits were the sign of demons. He would run to a safe distance and I would be spared.

Both prayers were answered, but neither had the effect I had hoped for. Jacob did not run. Perhaps in that moment it was hard to tell a fit from the thrashings and twistings of a woman fighting back.

Pain woke me. I was alone on the floor, naked. My thighs were sticky. I wiped at them and my hand came away covered with blood. I stood, but the pain made me double over and sink to my knees. I fell on hard coins. I picked them from my knees and stared at the citron, the ethrog, imprinted in them. Jacob had left the prostitute's fee. The coins would have seemed less horrible if they had been Greek drachmas or Roman denarii. But they were good Jewish bronze coins. The kind of coin Father used. The kind I played with as a child. I let them drop to the ground.

I had to get home, to Hannah and Judith. My ripped shift lay a body's length away. I crawled to it and began to wrap it around myself when the pain came again. I put both hands on my belly and held firm. I had to keep whole. I had to save Isaac. I fought the urge to scream. Isaac shouldn't hear me scream anymore.

A woman was with me when the blood came. My blood. The pool grew large. The pain knifed through me. I was on the floor again, writhing in the woman's arms, biting my own tongue to keep from screaming. My mouth filled with blood as the blood poured out between my legs. And I was pushing, just for a moment, so quickly it would have been a blessing if this had been a ready birth. The hot water that followed was almost a comfort.

The pain ceased.

I forced myself to sit up. Between my legs was Isaac. The woman lifted him from the ripped birth sac. She wiped him dry with my shift and gave my son to me. He was tiny; he fit in my cupped hands easily. But he was perfect. Ten miniature fingers. Ten miniature toes. His chin was pointed like his father 's. His legs were long, like mine. Even in death, even so tiny, I could see that he would have been a tower of a man. Who knows? He might have been a rabbi. He might have fought for our people, like a Hasid; he might have been in spirit a holy descendant of the heroes of the resistance against the Greeks. He might have been an heir to the prophetic tradition Judith talked so much of. Isaac, my laughter, quiet and cold in my hands.

I swaddled him in my shift. The prostitute draped her cloak around herself and me and we walked home in the brightest of moonlights. She curved in toward me, warbling words of comfort. And now I could see her as more than just the hands that had passed Isaac to me. She was an older woman, with her hair dyed Antioch-red to hide the ravages of time. Her cheeks and lips were likewise red from sikra. Even her palms were dyed a reddish yellow from the leaves of the privet, al khanna, that I knew of from the *Song of Songs.* I would have pulled away from her under any other circumstance. I would have avoided her as I avoided swine. But now I submitted to her warmth and colors. My nose was

assailed with her storax and gelbanum and ony-
cha and frankincense. Again I thought of the
strongly scented oils in the love canticles. This
prostitute owed me nothing; she knew me not at
all. Yet she freely helped a woman that she must
have expected to despise her. I grasped at her
generosity and a shiver shot through me. The
woman circled her arm around me and pulled
the cloak tighter. A ragged scar ran the length of
her left arm, from wrist to the inside of the
elbow. Her breath was thick with the fig-like
fruit of the sycamore, a fruit only the poor ate.
She was a woman alone, supporting herself, buying what foods she could afford. A woman of her
own means. A whore.

There was almost no one on the streets at that
hour. But those few men who passed us seemed
confused. They couldn't see Isaac within the
cloak. They knew nothing. The prostitute deliv-
ered me into the open hands of Judith and Hannah.

They washed me quietly and quickly, and
helped me to my bed mat. Judith knelt beside me
and whispered, "Tell me, Miriam."

What was there to tell? What mattered now? I looked around the room. Our bowls and plates were in order. Our chest of clothes was in place. The moonlight came in through the window. All was ordinary. This was a night like any other. No night would stand out from the others again. No day. "His name is Isaac," I said at last.

"A good name." Judith touched her fingers to my lips. "How did it happen, Miriam?"

I looked at her waiting face. She needed to know; there must have been a reason she needed to know. Maybe once I had known what that reason was, but now I couldn't remember. I told her, though, for her sake. I watched her cry.

Late that night I awoke to find Judith and Hannah and Father talking. At first they didn't want me to be part of the conversation. Then they relented and gathered me into their circle. They were discussing me, Miriam, the woman whom Jacob had seen trying to seduce an idiot boy. People didn't want to believe it. They all knew Father and liked him. Yes, he had a strange daughter, but that was all, just strange. Except for the fact which Jacob pointed out so coolly: It wasn't the first time. I had slept with Abraham, after all. It didn't take much to figure that out. And Abraham, too, was an idiot. I was now seen as a danger to the village. A woman whose lusts revealed her as a consort of the devil.

I sat stunned as I listened. I recognized nothing of the woman they discussed. Who was this stranger, this Miriam?

Father put his hand over mine. "It's all lies, Miriam. There are penalties for what Jacob has done, so he has found a way to stop anyone from believing you. He has even called upon the scriptures, twisting them to suit his own needs. He tells us all to remember Jacob's daughter Dinah, who provoked her assault by Shechem simply by going out to visit the daughters of the land. He stirs up the ancient feeling that a woman who appears in public is up to no good. He says you used to come by his shop to tease him — that you had tried to lure him before. He is scared, Miriam, and his fear makes him a formidable enemy." Father's hand tightened around mine. "I would kill him if it would matter."

I stared at Father. My humane father, speaking

of killing. And yet I wasn't sure I wouldn't kill Jacob myself if I could. Yes. In this moment I might have crushed Jacob as passionlessly as I crushed the insects that invaded the garden. I might have slit his throat and bled him like a butcher bleeds a goat.

"But it would not matter." Father shook his head. "For after Jacob there could well be another. And another." He stopped.

Another after Jacob? Unthinkable.

"Miriam." Father's voice was lifeless now. I knew his words to come would hurt him. I knew he feared they would hurt me, too. But they couldn't. Nothing could hurt me.

Father spoke: "You will not be safe in Magdala ever again."

It had happened. Finally. I was a pariah. After fearing it for so many years, it had happened — and not for the reasons I had expected. Not for my illness.

I should have been afraid then, for my future. I should have begun thinking of ways to hide. Instead, all I could do was wonder why the Creator hadn't permitted me to drown in my own saliva in that, my fifth fit. I didn't see the sense of going on living. Why would the Creator ask this of me? If Abraham had been there to talk to, perhaps I'd have found solace. Perhaps he'd have explained it to me patiently, as he had explained the use of the tools in Jacob's carpenter shop those many years ago. But Abraham wasn't there. And Judith and Hannah and Father seemed far away, though they sat close by on the floor. Everything seemed far away.

Isaac was gone forever.

CHAPTER ELEVEN

The journey to my mother's relatives in Dor was slow and hot. The arid land radiated heat. I rode in a cart pulled by oxen. Father sat beside me. Two of his laborers walked behind. They were not needed for work on this journey; they were there to ward off would-be highway robbers.

I had two aunts and an uncle in Dor. I'd never seen them. The journey's length would not have prohibited visits among close families, but ours had not been close, even when my mother was alive. I didn't know the story of the rift. Father was not one to talk a lot. But I knew there had been a rift. They hadn't come even for Mother's funeral. Father had hired a runner to transport Mother's harp to them.

The day before we left Magdala, Father sent a messenger ahead to my uncle. Judith had insisted I go to him, rather than an aunt, for my aunts were both married and I was beautiful. She feared the husbands of my aunts would want to take me for their second wife. I knew I could prevent that. All I had to do was tell them about the fits — the fits that neither Judith nor Father knew anything about. But I didn't speak up. For if Judith and Father knew of my fits, they'd have realized they couldn't send me to any relative. They'd have realized I'd be out in the streets with the other pariahs as soon as the next fit came. I wouldn't give them this problem.

So I would go to live with my mother's brother, if he would take me in. He had a wife and three children, at last count. I could help with the children. They were not rich; they had no servants. It would be an act of charity for them; I would be one more mouth to feed. That's why Hannah wasn't allowed to come along with me, though she pleaded. My uncle could not be asked to feed her, as well. Oh, he would be given money for taking me in, but he would still behave as though it was an act of largesse.

There would be no worry of my mother's brother wanting to take me for a wife, for though it was not forbidden that an uncle marry his niece, I looked so much like my mother, that Father was sure her own brother could not desire me.

I had no curiosity about my uncle. I had no curiosity about anything. My body still hurt. It had been only a week since I'd come home from the marketplace. Usually after the birth of a son the mother was unclean for forty days. But since Isaac had never breathed, his birth didn't count. So my unclean time was only the normal seven days for monthly blood. I was tired still and disoriented. I retreated within my body like a snail within a shell. I wanted no part of the plans for my future.

I was feverish for the first part of the trip. Father let us stay in an inn in the small town of Gaba until my fever broke. He couldn't very well ask my uncle to welcome an ill woman. I didn't seem to see Gaba. I was blind like the snail in the shell.

What should have been a day's journey for healthy people turned out to be a three-day trek. When we arrived at last, my uncle took me in. The messenger had done his job. "Welcome to

Thaddaeus' house," said my uncle with a great show of magnanimity.

Even in my stupor, I was surprised. My uncle called himself by the Greek deformation of the Hebrew name. It did not come easy to my mouth. I could not call him that. "Thank you, Uncle."

"You look like your mother. My home is your home."

My uncle's wife, Rachel, showed no joy at the prospect. I didn't realize until later that she blanched at my beauty, the beauty that meant nothing to me. I couldn't have consoled her, anyway. For she didn't fear that I would entice away my uncle from his wife. She knew from my dead eyes that I had no such intention. Instead, she feared that my beauty would make him realize her plainness that much more, and lead him to yearn for another, younger wife. There was nothing I could have said or done to soothe her.

The three children Father had spoken of were grown. Time passes, even when you don't see it going by. The two girls were already married. The only son, Samuel, was eleven already. No one needed my help. Father had to pay my uncle a great sum to take me, I knew that. He left, promising to send more money and to visit twice a year, bringing Judith along. But things conspired against us, and though the money came, Father and Judith never did.

I spent the next two years in my uncle's house, under the hawk eye of Rachel. I scrubbed and mended and carried water. I went to the well early, sometimes before sunrise, in order to avoid the women with children. Just as Hannah had avoided them years ago. But Hannah had avoided them so that they wouldn't object to Abraham, whereas I avoided them because I couldn't bear to see the babies.

I wouldn't let myself think about Isaac; I wouldn't let myself wonder what he'd be doing now if he had lived.

I was fervent in my household activities. I ground the grain and baked the bread. And most of all I kept at my woolwork, ever mindful that those around me considered woolwork the guardian of womanly virtue. I washed Uncle's feet when he came home at night. I rubbed his head and body with oil when he had worked in the sun. My size and strength were useful and I made Rachel's load lighter. But still she did not soften toward me. We rarely spoke, other than her giving orders and me answering questions.

I met both my mother's sisters. One was tall — not so tall as me, but taller than the average woman. Both were less than loving. Both suspected that I had done something shameful to have been sent here like this. They thought I'd been banished. I responded to their questions with the least information possible. I didn't ask which one of them had Mother's harp. I asked nothing. I never learned from them or Uncle why my mother had been so estranged from them. They never mentioned her name except the very first time they saw me, when they, like Uncle, proclaimed my resemblance to her. After the initial excitement passed, they stopped coming to visit.

Father sent money regularly, a purse to Uncle and a purse directly to me. It was a great sum he sent me and I wondered, if he was sending an equal sum to Uncle, what Uncle spent it on. For we certainly ate the simplest of meals — Rachel used only barley, never indulging in the more expensive wheat, the grain I was accustomed to having so often back home. I had always taken a certain pleasure in the coarseness of barley, though; it was in barley fields that Ruth of the scriptures went gleaning. But I knew Rachel chose barley not out of the dearness of Ruth, but out of the dearness of money.

And Rachel never bought a pretty dress. Once a peddler passed down our road on the way to market and Rachel eyed a purple cloth, embroidered intricately at the edges. It was a himation, a length of cloth to be wrapped round and round the body, with a portion that would hang loosely over the top of the head. Rachel owned nothing of such beauty. Her tight jaw showed how much she wanted it, but she didn't go inside for the money. I thought of buying it for her. After all, I, too, had once longed to clothe myself in dresses stained purple with the murex shellfish. But Rachel and I were not in the habit of doing kindnesses for one another and I was far from sure that she would welcome the act. It could be taken as flaunting.

I had nothing I wanted to spend my own

money on. The very feel of coins in my hand was hateful after the coins Jacob had left for me in the hall of prostitutes. But I was practical; I saved the coins Father sent in a box that I wrapped with the rags I used for my monthly blood. The rags were washed clean, of course, but, still, no one dared touch them but me. The taboo against blood was strong; my money was safe.

In that box, as well, were two treasures. One was the flute Judith had given me. I found it sewn in a fold in my cloak. In my daze I had left Magdala without belongings, but for the sack Hannah pressed upon me, in which the dress she had woven lay folded. I had no desire for objects. But when I discovered the flute in my cloak, my hands held it reverently. I didn't play it. But I kept it, clean and silent.

The other treasure was a very soft and wide skin belt that could crumple in the hand to the size of a pomegranate, that fruit that the cheeks of the beloved were compared to in the *Song of Songs*, that fruit that Abraham enjoyed so much, that Abraham had fed to me with such painstaking care, seed by seed.

I'd bought the belt in a shop in Dor only a

month after my arrival here. It was my comrade of sorts; it secured my secrets. I bought it immediately after my dreams began.

At first I didn't know what my dreams were about, I only knew I screamed and Rachel had to shake me that first time till I stopped. I was soaked in sweat and I couldn't catch my breath for many minutes. My head pounded with blood. My hands tingled with fear. I looked around, frantic to figure out where I was. And by the time I had, all memory of the dream had vanished. In the morning I put on my veil and went to the street of shops and bought the belt. That night I smoothed it flat over my mouth and tied it tight behind my head before I slept. In the dead of night I woke, my screams muffled in the belt. Every night thereafter I woke, silenced behind the belt.

After a while I could remember the dreams. They all started out in a different activity, but they all ended the same. I would be walking someplace beautiful I didn't recognize, or milling grain in happy anticipation of a feast whose purpose I didn't know, or embroidering a cloth for a person I'd never met. I would always be happy and always be busy and always be looking forward to something good, something new and wonderful and unknown. Then a man would come and invite me away. I knew I shouldn't go, but I couldn't help it. He needed me to come. His need was urgent. And when I went to him, he became Jacob. He threw me down and raised a rock and smashed my hands, one then the other, crushed every bone until they were bloody stumps. Then he raised the rock again to smash my feet, but I had already awoken myself with my screams.

I felt my hands, the length of each finger, over and over and over. I assured myself they were still useful. My womanly virtue persisted as long as my fingers were whole, as long as they could still do woolwork. I stared at the oil lamp, burning feebly in the closed night air of Uncle's home, and thought of nothing. Eventually sleep recaptured me.

I learned after a few months that I could take the skin belt off my mouth after a dream, for the dream never returned again in the same night. It was a small kindness, that.

I went to the house of prayer often. I wore a

veil and I dressed in black, as I had since Abraham's death. But I was a noticeable figure, all the same. Eyes followed me. It didn't take long before the offers of marriage came. I told Uncle I was barren. Father had suggested something of the sort to him, though I believed Father had managed to keep from lying outright. And so Uncle fended off the suitors and I kept my day full, between work and the house of prayer.

Rachel's eyes turned inquisitive at my revelation of being barren. There was only one way a woman could know such a thing. Rachel wanted to ask about the man who used to be in my life. She fingered my black shift and looked sly. There was no reason for a widow to go live with her mother's relatives. If I had been married, why wasn't I living now with people I cared about? With my husband's relatives or my own father? And why did I wear no ring? I could see Rachel's mouth grow dry with desire to ask. Had her eyes shown the slightest hint of sympathy, I might have confided in her. I longed for the confidences of women. I missed Judith's sensible strength that gave such force to her love. I missed Hannah's thin, quick fingers that knew how to ease pain. But Rachel's eyes were cold and cunning. It was curiosity born of the chance that maybe she could have power against me. Maybe she could discredit me and be rid of me. So I stayed aloof and found excuses to leave the house whenever she came to me with that expectant look on her face. Perhaps I cheated us both. But the risk was too great to take.

Once I woke from a dream to find Rachel sitting beside me, watching, her eyes like a jackal's in the dim light of the lamp. I rolled on my side and waited till she returned to her own bed mat. I told myself there was no crime in bad dreams. She could use them for nothing. Still, I began a regimen of barley soaked in curdled milk and a spoonful of honey before I went to sleep. Anything to stay the severity of those dreams. I don't know whether those remedies helped or if it was simply the effect of time, but by my second winter in Uncle's home, though the dreams still came, I suffered less from them, because after a dream I fell asleep almost immediately.

Or perhaps it was the mercy of the Creator that reduced my suffering. For I was not proud in asking Him for mercy.

I went to the house of prayer more and more often, sometimes twice in a day. Once when I was walking there, panic overcame me. It was as though I had lost something, something important, something precious. My arms ached to hold that something. I walked ever faster, letting my eyes search the side alleys. I ran. I had to find it or disaster would strike. But then the panic left and I knew again that Isaac was dead. I knew he lay quiet in the shallow grave beside his father. I walked slowly once again.

This house of prayer, though I felt compelled to go there, was not a place of pleasure for me. I never went when the Levites were there. I didn't want to hear singing. I went at odd hours. I stood in the rear, and listened to the silence, and thought. When song is gone, when words are gone, all that remains are tears and silence. But I was dry as the land. So silence was my altar.

The house of prayer was a small place of worship, smaller than the house of prayer in Magdala. I liked its smallness. I wanted the world to be small and dark and safe. When I was outside the house of prayer, my breath was lost in the vastness of the world. But when I stood inside, I could almost believe my breath had substance again. I could almost hear it reverberate.

Though the house of prayer had become my private place, it was, in fact, the most public of places. Everyone in town came here, not just to worship, but to exchange information. And try though I might to come when others were less likely to be around, I found myself inevitably passing through the doorway as a group was passing in the other direction. Once I became a familiar sight, they no longer ceased their talk as we passed. I came to hear snatches of conversation, snatches that gradually tantalized me.

My life until that point had been like a closed fist. I knew my home, my family, my Abraham. I wasn't part of the gossip at the well in Magdala. I had heard when Herod Antipas built Tiberias so near to Magdala, yes; still the news meant little to me in my family world then. Now in Dor I had no real home. So the larger world crept up on me, sneakily, loosening my fingers, seeking my palm.

Dor was a coastal town brimming with Romans and Greeks, energized with the sound of drachmas exchanging hands. The spirit of the town was diverse. The pagans had their gods; the

Jews had another. But everyone met amicably over trade. Or, if not amicably, profitably. This I learned from the talk at the well.

I changed my habits: I now went to the well when the most people would be there, just so I could hear more talk. I learned there that Dor's successful Jewish merchants called themselves by pagan names like Phillip and Andrew. I saw Uncle's aspirations in calling himself Thaddaeus. And I knew very well that he'd never realize those aspirations — for his business acumen was dull. The women talked of exotic foods in the marketplace, too. I never went to the market, of course. The hall of prostitutes was bound to be near there. But my own eyes witnessed the horses that the non-Hebrews rode, magnificent creatures, so much taller than the donkey of every Jewish household. Yes, Dor was a place of ambition and excitement.

But it was a place of discontent, as well. News passed from mouth to mouth, like shared bread. The Romans' demands for taxes had grown intolerable. There was a land tax payable in produce or money. There was an income tax. There was a poll tax for everyone but children and the aged. And there was a custom duty tax on imports from each Roman province. Those who tried to avoid paying were imprisoned or flogged by the Roman military.

David, the tax collector for my section of Dor, was hated. He was a Jew; he held our history heavy within his heart, like the rest of us. He knew that before the Romans there were the Greeks, the Babylonians, the Assyrians, the Egyptians. Our invaders went back so far — perhaps forever. History had taught us over and over that periods of self-rule came to an end. Though the pagans who walked the streets of Dor lived in peace with the people of Israel today, David knew, like the rest of us, that such cooperation was transitory. So he had to know that working for the Romans now could come to no good end. Yet David bid for the job of tax collector. The highest bidder got the job and earned our hatred. The other bidders were forgiven and accepted back as though they had never strayed.

Now and then I'd see David at the house of prayer. Once I walked up behind him as he prayed. I moved on flat feet, with no attempt to conceal the sound of flesh on stone. Yet I felt stealthy. I had the sensation of stalking. My skin prickled. I was going to ask him if he came to beg for the Creator's forgiveness. I was going to ask him what the source of desperation was in his life, for his acts were the acts of a desperate man. I waited for his prayer to end, when suddenly he turned and looked at me before I had a chance to open my mouth. He walked quickly past me, out of the house of prayer.

An enormous tension released inside me. I sank to the floor, as though my bones had turned to water. What had taken hold of me? I had almost talked to this stranger. I looked around. No one had seen. I stood up and smoothed my clothing with both hands. I touched the edges of my veil. No hair escaped from under it. I was a proper woman. I must behave always as a proper woman. Oh, yes, Hannah was right to have all her extra private laws about what colors to ban and how to wear veils. Nothing was more important than appearing proper, than drawing no attention.

At the well I blended in with the other women. I kept my eyes lowered and listened closely. I heard the history of Pontius Pilate, the Roman governor of Palestine. When Pilate first came to Jerusalem, he brought troops carrying army standards with images of the Roman gods. Pilate knew nothing about the Judeans he was sent to rule. He had never heard of our Second Commandment, which forbade false images of the Creator. Either that, or he knew very well precisely what he was doing — he planned every insult. Our people rebelled. They offered their necks to the Roman swords, preferring to die than to see our laws disdained.

Oh, how I wished I could have seen those crowds. I'd have cheered for the men. And, maybe, given how foolish I was four years ago, when Pilate caused that rebellion, maybe I'd have offered my own neck, joining with the men where women never tread.

Pilate relented and finally removed the religious standards. But that didn't mean he'd learned anything. He was biding his time. Until just months ago, when he confiscated money from the Temple in Jerusalem. No pagan should have touched the sacred money. Again crowds gathered in that holy city, crowds of valiant Jews. Pilate sent his soldiers in with weapons concealed in their garments. At an agreed upon signal, they drew their swords and massacred everyone. The Jews of Jerusalem were decimated.

Fear radiated out from Jerusalem to every city and village. Anger followed. Even here in peaceful Dor the word on everyone's lips was *freedom*. People were willing to leave much to Rome as long as they had freedom to follow the laws of our ancestors. But the Romans were too stupid or too mean or both. They denied us what they could so easily have allowed. In some villages our people couldn't even buy meats slaughtered properly, so they ate only bread and vegetables and fruits.

Initially the higher taxes were to blame for Father and Judith's not visiting me. For as desperation increased, highway robbery became almost a daily occurrence. No one traveled without multiple guards, and then only when absolutely necessary. Later it was the talk of rebellion that kept them away. The Romans took to stopping groups of travelers and turning them back in an effort to quell trouble before it began. I missed Father and Judith and Hannah terribly. I had my own private reason for wanting Pilate's downfall.

And so the talk in Dor was ever more important to me. The men's words turned to whispers now. I'd pretend to be tired and rest on the steps of the house of prayer, close to a huddle of men. But they whispered so softly, I couldn't hear them anymore, no matter how hard I strained. I knew they talked of revolt.

My dreams turned to my own kind of personal revolt. After my nightmare each night, new and marvelous dreams came. I dreamed of Jerusalem, a city I had never seen. Abraham came to me. He spoke quietly, with the words of the fifth canticle:

> I sleep, but my heart waketh: it is the voice of my beloved that knocketh, saying, Open to me my sister, my love, my dove, my undefiled: for my head is filled with dew, and my locks with the drops of the night.

I arose eagerly and walked the streets of Jerusalem without a veil and without fear. Abraham walked with me. He was not tall or beautiful or straight in anyone's eyes but mine. He was my wonderful Abraham. He told the crowds that the scriptures spoke not of our history, but of the here and now, of how we, the people known as Israel, must live today. He said the lessons were there if only we would heed them. He said Pontius Pilate was a fool. He said Herod Antipas was no one's true leader. He said we must care for one another, the infirm and the whole, side by side.

In the mornings I woke with Abraham's words in my mouth. But I was not the Miriam I had been. I swallowed his words. I was a proper woman.

I walked by the beggars in the street, dropping a coin in every open hand I passed. But I never looked in their faces, I never listened to their pleas. They had nothing to do with me. Nothing moved me but the instinct for self-preservation. I was a proper woman.

I woke each day with no hopes of anything new and I went to sleep tired of body. My soul didn't have the courage to fight. I was like the men on the steps of the house of prayer, full of whispers and sighs. I was like the women at the well, preaching only to the converted, getting nowhere. Revolt was no more in my real plans than it was in theirs. If Abraham's uncle Daniel had died in Alexandria, his Zealot's spirit was surely buried with him, for none I knew breathed the spirit of rebellion in the air of this world.

Rachel never stopped expecting something new from me, though what I cannot guess. Some revelation of my past, perhaps. Or maybe she was more attuned than I knew — maybe she could sense the source of my fits in the deep nightmare hollows beneath my eyes. She watched me carefully, no matter how mundane a chore I performed. And it was her careful watching that finally brought about the change I lacked the energy to bring about myself.

I was hanging the laundry before dawn so that I could go to the house of prayer early. Just the day before I had heard the tail end of a story about a man named Jochanan, who preached repentance and welcomed the despised of society: the tax collectors, the rough soldiers, the prostitutes, the cripples. I had to hear more. Oh yes, I had to hear more. The Pharisees of Dor, our most respected people, were planning on going to visit him. I wanted to know where this Jochanan was and what moved him.

As I hung each article of clothing, tension gripped my middle. If the Creator saw fit to ruin a woman's family — unless shelter was offered to her, unless work was extended to her, unless the community protected her — that woman, any woman, could become a prostitute. Any woman at all. Any one of us. If the Creator saw fit to wither our limbs, to crush our spines, to twist our bodies, we, too, would be cripples and, thus, beggars. Any man, woman, or child. Any one of us. This Jochanan welcomed prostitutes. He welcomed cripples. Did he understand? Was there finally a man speaking the truth? My fingers worked faster and faster. I was crazy to know more of this Jochanan. When I finished, I pressed my face into the wet cloth of Uncle's hanging shirt and breathed the comfort of damp air. In these dry days, damp air was as a treasure. My heart beat violently.

The sixth fit came. I knew because the knot in

the pit of my stomach compressed my insides painfully to a small chunk of marble. The light was exquisite. I clutched Uncle's shirt and in my spasms, I grasped the line. The clean wash fell, as I fell. In the dust.

I didn't sleep, unlike in the past. I lay quiet, spent, with the realization upon me that I was, indeed, still Miriam the Magdalene, the infirm — that no matter how I closed my eyes to misery, it still existed in this world. The beggars were there; their existence did not rely on my acknowledgement. The world was out there and I was in here and every little thing overwhelmed me. I was powerless.

And then I heard Rachel screech behind me. "*Shedim*! Devils! You are possessed!"

I hadn't pictured this moment, I hadn't prepared for it, yet I found myself speaking with calm authority, as I stood up. "Rachel, call my uncle. Quickly. Do as I say."

The fear in Rachel's eyes would have wounded me if we had ever become friends. As it was, I was grateful — for Rachel obeyed.

I brushed the dust from my arms and hair. I

must have thrashed more violently this time, for my shift was rent.

Uncle came outside, pulling his shirt over his head, dressing as he walked. His face was wary. Disbelief struggled with fear. "What is it, Miriam?"

"What Rachel has told you is true." I paused, to let the import of my words sink in. My uncle's face grew still. "I'm going away, Uncle. I will cause no harm to you or your family so long as you do one favor for me."

My uncle's mouth hung open. He had never bargained with devils before.

Rachel moved slightly behind my uncle. "What favor?"

The urge to hiss, to howl, left my jaw clenched. I could have slit my wrist with the useful knife tucked in my cloth belt. I could have sprayed their mouths with my blood and told them they had drunk of an evil that would live within them forever. But what use was there in venting my anger on their withered souls? They were pitiful. If I had any pity in me, none would have deserved it more than Uncle and Rachel. I spoke softly. "Send a message to Father and Judith and Hannah. Tell them I've gone south to live."

Uncle lifted his chin. If he sent such a message, the money from Father would cease to come. He took a tentative step forward. "South? Where? Where will you go?"

Until that point I wasn't sure. I had thought of running away to Egypt to join the Therapeutae, a celibate society. I had thought of going to Jerusalem to trace the footsteps of the famous Huldah. I had even thought of trying to live as a hermit hidden in Father's valley. But now I realized I knew where I was heading, there was no doubt in my mind. When I was ten and the first fit came, I thought immediately of Qumran. The people at Qumran passed their days in prolonged prayer. They fasted and renounced the pleasures of this world. Those people would never take me in; I was not an Essene. But no one could keep me from the caves. And somehow I was sure that the caves themselves were holy. I would go to the caves at Qumran and live as a hermit. I was not brave enough to face the misery of this world, but I would no longer try to live within society and deny that misery.

Still, my family, Father and dear Judith and patient Hannah, none of them should know this. They would only mourn my loss and my choice. They might even try to find me. "Jerusalem," I said, speaking the holy name with reverence. "Tell them not to come looking, for I am traveling with my husband."

"Your husband?" My uncle looked so confused that for a moment I was sure he was a stupid man. He did not know that the lie of marriage was the only way I could bestow upon my family any sense of peace. "Who is your husband?"

"Belial, the spirit of darkness," whispered Rachel.

My husband. My husband was not of this world. "Listen to Rachel," I said loudly. "She has seen what you have not. Tell them, Uncle. Tell Father and Judith and Hannah." And then I indulged in an empty threat — for I had no power to truly harm Uncle and I never would, even if I could have — but he had the power to harm the ones I loved, if he failed to pass on this message. "If you care for your family, if you care for your son Samuel, do as I say. Exactly as I say."

My uncle nodded slowly.

"He will," said Rachel firmly. "I swear he will."

I went into the house and changed into the best dress I had, the one Hannah had woven for me when I was only a girl. I would not go in mourning any longer. Abraham and Isaac had both been dead for more than two years. It was time to begin the rest of my life, whatever it should be. I gathered my few belongings, tucking my now heavy box of money in a drawstring cloth bag tied to the belt around my waist and hidden beneath the folds of my cloak. My quieted flute graced that bag, as well. The day was hot, yet I wanted that cloak to surround me, as though it were my traveling home, my tent. As though I were an Idumean, like the ancestors of the tyrannical and pitiless Herod the Great himself. I would appear formidable to all eyes.

I left by foot, without looking back.

CHAPTER TWELVE

Walking across the country to the River Jordan was an undertaking for young, strong men. Yet I knew I could do it. All those years of lifting Abraham and wandering with him had enabled me. People in carts passed, some offering words of caution, some asking if I needed assistance, some silent. I kept my face covered with my veil and walked with purpose, eyes straight ahead. I had a destination and I cared for no one's help or interference.

But my destination changed. For the very first night on the road, I stopped at a small country home and begged lodging in their barn. I had money upon me. Yet I offered none. I realized that if I made it known I had money, I might soon find myself without it. I still practiced self-preservation.

The farmer and his family were gracious. They shared their bread and creamy soft cheeses with me. They had used no part of the calf to curdle those cheeses. Their strict interpretation of the dietary laws impressed me and I gave thanks for finding myself at a decent table. In the morning I helped the older daughter feed the animals and clean out their stalls before I went on my way. It was she who changed my path.

When she heard I was going to the river, her eyes opened wide. "Are you going to be immersed?"

I was taken aback. If I were unclean, if I were in need of the mikvah, I certainly wouldn't have asked for lodging in their home. And other than the unclean, the only ones who underwent total immersion in water were pagans converting to Judaism. But I was not a pagan. What had I done to make this child think I was? "I am a Jewish woman."

The girl nodded enthusiastically, her wavy hair swinging about like fluttering wings. "A prostitute. You are, aren't you? Mother guessed that. She said your dress showed you were a woman of means, and since you were alone, it had to be from your own earnings. She said she never would have allowed you in, but for your eyes." The girl breathed hard. "I've heard Jochanan baptizes prostitutes all the time." Her voice was rapid with excitement. Her eyes glittered wet. "Some would hate you. But I agree with Mother; your eyes look sad to me. The Creator be with you."

I walked away, looking over my shoulder often. But the girl didn't follow me. I was on the road toward a man named Jochanan who baptized prostitutes. It had to be the same Jochanan I had heard of in Dor. The man who called for repentance and welcomed the dregs of society. So this Jochanan baptized the people who came to him. As though their purification was as drastic a change in life as a pagan's undergoing conversion. This Jochanan was dramatic. An extremist. I understood the forces that made one become an extremist. My step quickened.

By late afternoon, I realized the road did not lead directly to the river. If I wanted the shortest path, I had to leave the road and cross the wilderness. I had taken my fill of water a few hours before. This was the end of the second day of what a more seasoned fellow foot traveler had told me would be just a three-day walk. I could certainly manage one day in the wilderness without water.

I left the road. Twilight was brief here; darkness overflowed the land almost as soon as the sun sank beneath the horizon. And with the vanishing of the light came the swift and piercing cold that loved the night. I walked deep into the blue-black air, hugging my cloak around me. It must have been midnight when I stopped to sleep. The stars filled the sky in every direction. They illuminated the immensity of this world. And if this world was so immense and wondrous, how much better must be the next. I sang that night, for the first time since Isaac's birth and death. I sang,

Whither is thy beloved gone, O thou fairest among women? whither is thy beloved turned aside? that we may seek him with thee.

My beloved is gone down into his garden, to the beds of spices, to feed in the gardens, and to gather lilies.

I am my beloved's and my beloved is mine: he feedeth among the lilies.

And I cried. I had never cried after Abraham or Isaac. But now, with the stars coming down to the earth all around me, I cried. The wilderness could give me no water, but I gave it my tears.

The stars waited just beyond my fingertips until I slept.

In the morning, I woke stiff and achy to the rosy dawn. I had slept solid. No nightmare had interrupted my regular breathing. My mouth was empty, wordless; the dream of Abraham, as well, had not come.

I knew I should rise, and quickly, too, for the sun would heat the earth mercilessly before long. Yet I stared at a small monitor who blinked back at me. I had slept in my shoes to keep the scorpions out and the warmth in. But now I looked about for scorpions, wishing to see them. I wanted to know the creatures that thrived here, so far from humans. I wanted to learn from them. And most of all, I wanted to see again that starry sky, wrapped in the silence of my cloak. I wanted nothing but starry nights alone till my end should come. I sat with my knees bent to my chest and my arms holding them close. I was motionless as the monitor.

I waited.

The monitor left. A gray gecko came. Then went. I thought of Moses' forty days upon Sinai. I thought of the days when Elijah went to Horeb. I wished I had gone further before I stopped, south to the desert — where I could dry out and become like air. Yet this wilderness would do.

I thought of the noisy doves in Mother's terebinth tree. I thought of my blood and how it would disappear in this parched dirt. I thought of Abraham's soft, tawny beard. My scattered thoughts dusted the hours.

My eyes played along the tracks of a lynx that had obviously come close in the night. I knew the lynx from Galilee, of course. But I'd never actually seen one myself — just tracks. Mother once told me cats were Egyptian in spirit. These tracks looked only solitary.

After a long while I parted my lips. From deep in my throat came a clear melody. I felt its wholeness, but I could barely hear it. Among the stars last night my song had seemed to carry forever. But in the sun it was lost. There was no wind that morning, none at all — yet my song was gone, absorbed in the ochre earth perhaps. Or perhaps I had fooled myself; perhaps I had produced no song now. I cupped my palms over my ears and sang again. Yes, there it was. Within me. It could not be heard in this wilderness.

I stood up. I took the balled-up skin belt from where I had tucked it away — that skin belt that had helped silence my night cries in Dor. I let it fall to the ground. I had no further use for silence.

I walked all the rest of that day. At times the heat shimmered, wavy-like, luring me from my true direction. But I always steered back to the line toward water. I felt neither thirst nor hunger. I was not tired. I was hot. Baked. I was sure my cloak was the only reason my skin didn't split from the heat.

I knew when I was close, for travelers began to appear, coming from south and north as well as west, like me. They greeted each other quickly and without ceremony. I saw holy men pass by, all going to a single destination. The Sadducees were easy to recognize: Their garments spoke of their wealth. Blue tassels swung from the bottom of their chalouks. I'd heard the villagers at Dor say the Sadducees were aligned with Rome. They led the easy life of privilege and comfort. They moved ahead as though it were their right.

The slower ones of us formed a kind of comradely group, following like the sheep that moved in thick flocks from one pasture to another around the hills of Galilee. Which of us was the shepherd? Which of us would spout prophecies like Amos or poems like David of the scriptures? Which of us was responsible for guarding against the hyena, the jackal, the wolf, even the bear? I felt like a sheep myself, all thick and stuffy in my wool cloak. Where would I be when the first rains of Heshvan came and the sheep were put under cover to pass the cold months?

The people around me talked of Jochanan the Baptist. I listened and gratefully accepted the food they shared, the food Jochanan told people must be shared. All must give to their neighbors. So Jochanan had been well named: He preached the Creator's graciousness and mercy, in accord with the meaning of his name. I thought again of the fiery prophet Amos, who said the Creator wanted not sacrifices, but decency and kindnesses among people. I wished I had something to give to these new neighbors of mine. But these people did not hold their hands outstretched and open for a coin, and all I had were useless coins.

Soon the sounds of many people made themselves heard. The travelers headed down the incline to the river ahead. The crowd slipped away, leaving me behind. I stopped at the top and sat to watch. My life was totally in my own hands for the first time; I would measure and judge my actions carefully.

A young man stood in the water, up to his knees, clad only in a garment of rough camel's hair. He wore a belt of skins. I recognized the apparel: He was dressed like the prophet Elijah, who had come to warn all Israel generations before, the prophet I had thought of only this morning. People believed Elijah would return before the day when the Creator would rescue His chosen people. Did this young man fancy himself to be Elijah? He was unkempt and bearded. He was skin and bones. The travelers said he ate only wild locusts, calling upon all to return to the diet people had in the days before the great flood. He preached the virtues of a gentler age.

But as I watched, I didn't see a gentle man. Jochanan railed at the Sadducees. He sent them away. And in the same breath, he welcomed the sinners, all of them, everywhere.

I wanted to join forces with this Baptist, for I realized in that moment that I, too, harbored anger. Oh, yes, rage. If I had screamed my rage right then, I would have deafened the whole world. Jochanan was right. I wanted to run to the Baptist and wade in the water and be purged. I wanted to welcome sinners, side by side with him.

Yet I held back.

There were women in the water. Some of them naked. They threw their heads about, their hair twirling round like halos. They moved to the chants of the men. The late sun glistened off the drops of water on their breasts and bellies.

Some of the men watched them openly. Others gave the appearance of not caring, yet their stances were unnatural. Every man there was aware of the sweetness of fruit. I watched and listened; oh, how I listened.

But the women didn't sing.

Not a single female voice rode the air. The separateness of women made itself known even here.

I would never stand in that water — no matter how cleansing and cool and rejuvenating it might be — and keep my songs inside. I had given up my songs twice. I would never give them up again. The stars of the wilderness night had returned them to my mouth. And oh they were sweeter in my mouth than any fruit these men or women here could ever offer. My songs were me and I was them. Jochanan was a leader to follow, but I was not looking for a leader to follow. I wasn't looking to follow anyone.

I stood up and walked along the ridge, southward. I walked parallel to the river for several hours, with fertile, low-lying valleys to both sides. I passed a clump of tamarisks, growing thick and giving welcome cool. Their sprays of pink flowers had long since passed, yet the air was pungent. It was complete night when I finally descended to the River Jordan and drank. Jochanan and all his baptized were now far behind. I held my hands and wrists in the shallow waters until my blood ran cool again. The jackals howled; the hyenas laughed harshly. I slept by the water.

In the morning I continued southward, always following the winding riverbed, passing myrrh and nettles and now and then a bed of papyrus growing in the water. I saw the hoofprints of antelopes and gazelles. A Sinai ibex picked its way along the water's edge.

Food was not a problem, for I met many who were traveling north to see the Baptist. They shared their food with me. I did small tasks in return. I rubbed tired shoulders and repaired broken sandals.

I walked for days. The land dropped in altitude. I could feel the press of the air, as though I weighed more the lower the land got. As though I was being pulled to the center of the earth. The land was now rows of red silt, as red as the cliffs on the east side of my own Sea of Galilee. I passed Idumean nomadic camps that seemed as timeless as the river. I was careful not to let them see me, just as the antelopes had been careful not to let me see them, for their people and mine had been enemies for generations. The air was hot and thick and heavy.

On the fourth day travelers told me Jericho was off to the west. I looked and saw the outline of the city that held the splendid palace Herod the Great had built. I remembered the roses from Jericho that Abraham and I had smelled in the market so long ago. I remembered savoring the thickness of rose petals. Was every house ornamented with a rose garden? Did oleanders overhang every wall, willows grace every well? I turned and looked across the river valley to the grand Moab mountains, rich in palm trees and balm. I thought of the wonderful woman Ruth, a Moabite, the first convert to Judaism. Ruth had traveled and changed her life for love.

Entreat me not to leave thee, or to return from following after thee: for whither thou goest, I will go; and where thou lodgest, I will lodge: thy people shall be my people, and thy God my God.

I had known a love as strong as Ruth's. I would have gone with Abraham wherever he beckoned.

I walked with renewed vigor. The Jordan widened and grew muddy among reeds and the ever-present willows. Finally I came out to the lowest point in our land, the Dead Sea.

The Dead Sea was flat, with water thick like skin. The yellow cliffs beyond rose straight up to the Creator's sky. The air filled my ears, pressed on my eardrums, making me know a silence that was more majestic and beautiful than any I could have imagined. It was as though the silence of the small house of prayer in Dor had multiplied and spread and given peace to the world. I could imagine a perfect understanding as I sat there. For the first time I understood the vows of silence that some holy people take.

In the morning I walked the short distance left to Qumran. The community that Father had once seen stood on a white terrace of marl, many feet above the road. A high tower rose on one side of the thick walls. I reached my hands toward it instinctively. No child of Magdala could help being drawn to that tower.

On the seaside stretched out an immense cemetery with row after row of graves. A mound of stones, lined up north to south, marked each grave. I marveled. No other Jews I knew of, nor pagans, either, lined up their graves like that. I was happy at the mystery. I had no need to understand.

I lived in the caves of the hills near Qumran for many moons. Some of the caves were high, so that when I stood at the mouth and looked out, I felt I could step into the heavens and fly. Some had openings at the top so that at night I could stare up at the stars. Some had walls smooth to the touch, as though they'd been worn down by thousands of groping fingers over thousands of years. From my favorite cave, I looked south and saw hill interleaving with hill, forming a crisscross valley dotted with the mouths of caves.

The cave I inhabited was none of these. It was low, opening in a gradual decline to level ground. There were no holes in the roof. It was solid and protective. It sat on the north edge of the cave hills, closest to a town.

I bought food at a farm on the edge of that town. The farmer, unquestioning, took my money and treated me fairly.

Once, before the start of the cold weather, it

rained hard for three days and three nights. Water ran in rivulets on both sides of the opening of my cave. It splashed against the stones. I was astonished. I'd been told this land was parched.

Then the rain ceased. It didn't slow down and taper off. It simply vanished. And the sky stretched clear and blue-white. I stepped out of my cave and walked paths strewn with pebbles washed there from the downpour. The light off the wet, white pebbles broke into colors. The world was as bright as before one of my fits. I thought I could see forever. And I remembered, all at once, the great happiness colors had given me as a child.

Besides that rain, those months were without incident, night as well as day. The dream of Jacob that had plagued me in Dor had died in the wilderness. I was alone. I took to wearing my veil constantly, so that if by chance a stranger should see me, no one would question that I was a proper woman. Yet I knew that precaution was needless; the white rocks and caves were free of others' spirits.

So I passed my days in worshipful devotion to the Creator, trying to learn His holy plan. One day I spied something pink just below the water surface at the edge of the Dead Sea. I put in my hand and seized a slippery stone the size of Abraham's fist. I brought it home and held it as I sat, hour after hour, day after day, month after month. I turned it and rubbed it and thought over the events of my life. I sought a reason. I pressed the stone to my cheek, I breathed my inner heat over it and watched the condensation on the coldest mornings. I rubbed and rubbed and rubbed it. The pink must have been a thin coating of mineral deposit, for it wore off with my rubbing, exposing the marl beneath. My constant polishing made the white glow. Yet I grew no wiser. I prayed to the Creator more passionately. I stood on tiptoe to be closer to the Creator. I pressed both hands as if in a hood sticking out from my eyebrows to concentrate better. I overflowed with energy. I was ready. I was Miriam, beloved of the Creator, I was ready to fulfill the destiny of my name. Every moment of every day, I was ready, my stone cupped in both hands.

Then one day I heard a woman singing. At first I thought I imagined it, it seemed but a memory of a song that perhaps I had sung myself the week before or maybe a month before. But the song continued, high and keening, wordless sounds that brought tears to my eyes. I tucked my stone into my belt and went in search. I climbed among the cliffs, following a sound that echoed deceptively here and there, until I finally found her, at the mouth of a low cave I knew well, with her girl child in her lap. The child was listless. The woman hushed as soon as she saw me.

"Go on, sing," I said.

She stared at me.

"Sing!" I touched the girl's forehead as her mother sang a song in a tongue I didn't speak. The girl's eyes were bright with fever — not raging like Abraham's when he first fell ill — but present and steady and relentless. It sapped her energy.

I thought immediately of the oily waters of the Dead Sea, the waters that reeked of mineral decay, the waters whose buoyancy I had struggled against these months when I called upon the sea to serve as my mikvah. They might have healing powers, and they surely would cool her down. I reached for the child. "Let's soak her in the sea."

The woman looked at me. "That helps only

temporarily. Within the hour, the fever returns."
She spoke Hebrew in an accent unfamiliar to me.
It lured me.

I dropped my outstretched arms, unwilling to
be lured. "What causes it?"

"I don't know." The mother spoke in a whisper, as though the child wouldn't hear her that
way, even though the child lay in her arms,
within breath's reach. "I came for help from the
people at Qumran. I want to take her to Galilee.
But no one will accompany me. And I don't have
the strength to carry her all that way myself."

Galilee. Magdala was in Galilee. "Why would
you go to Galilee?"

The woman looked at me as though my question was silly. She shook her head and her loose
black hair brushed the child's legs. "So she can
be cured."

I crossed my arms at the chest and hugged myself. A woman who sought cures could not seduce me so easily. I would not yield so easily, no.
"Surely there are healers closer by. Jerusalem is
much closer than Galilee."

"I have been to healers. So many Roman healers."

I bent over her, wondering if I had heard right. "Roman?"

"I am not a Jew like you." She fingered the edge of my veil and looked me up and down. "I am Roman."

A pagan. I had suspected she was pagan, yet to hear her say it gave a sting. I straightened up. In Magdala we kept our distance from the pagan women. They did not even come to the same well. Some said they did not drink water at all, only wine.

"But do not be deceived. I would not limit myself to Roman healers." The woman's voice was heavy with disappointment. "I have been to Jewish healers, Greek and Hellene healers. But no one can help. And many are unkind to a woman alone, even with a child." She looked at me meaningfully. "You must know how it is. A Jewish woman knows as well as a Roman woman." Her eyes insisted.

Were my eyes responding to that insistence against my will? I shut them.

She sighed loudly. "So I must get to Galilee. The great healer is there."

My eyes flew open. I shook my head in confusion. "I used to live in a town of Galilee. I knew of no great healer."

"He's only started healing in the last few months. But he can heal everyone. He's cured blindness, lameness, paralysis, catalepsy, hemorrhage, wounds. All those things have to be harder to cure than my daughter's fever, don't you agree?" The woman clutched my skirt with her hand, just like Abraham used to clutch my shift. "They say he has raised the dead. Now that has to be much harder than curing my baby's fever, don't you agree?"

I hardly heard her last words. I kept repeating the first few in my head. Paralysis. This healer cured paralysis? I felt suddenly scared for the first time in a very long while. My trembling fingers played on my wide belt where I had tucked the polished stone. Everything I owned was on my body. I was intact. Yet I felt as though I'd lost something, left something behind. "What is this healer's name?"

"Your people call him Joshua, son of Miriam."

The son of Miriam. Isaac would have been called the son of Miriam, too. I stroked my dry throat. My skin jangled at the touch of my own hand. I no longer resisted. "Do you sing often?"

The woman looked down at her daughter, who had fallen asleep in her arms. She whispered, "Singing helps relieve the pain."

I leaned over the child and watched her long lashes flutter on her flushed cheeks. "Yes," I said softly. Our whispers mingled with the hot breath of the sleeping child. "But why would a Roman woman seek help from the Essenes at Qumran? Surely your own people will take you to Galilee."

"No Roman would help me."

A woman whose own people wouldn't help her. I sat down beside her. "Why not?"

"They hate Joshua."

"They hate a healer?"

"He's not just a healer. The people claim he is the son of God."

"All Jews are the children of the Creator. So he is Jewish, then?"

"Yes. But he isn't meek like the other Jews. Some say he's dangerous."

"Why?"

"The Jews flock to him. They believe him.

They are beginning to say he is their real king, not Caesar."

"King of the Jews," I said slowly. "So men go to him."

"Multitudes. And some travel with him."

"And he refuses no one?"

"He takes even idiots, the despised of society."

My heart skipped a beat. The fierce shouts of the prophet Amos were heard across the centuries, condemning those who would ignore the poor and needy. The cool, soothing words of Hillel rang out, affirming what we had to do. And now these new voices joined in. First Jochanan the Baptist and, finally, this Joshua. Would that he were a worthy heir to the tradition. "If he's way up in Galilee, how do you know so much about him?"

"He's been to Jerusalem. He's been everywhere. Everyone knows about him. He preaches that all are welcome and I know that all come."

All? "Do women come?"

"Not many, I don't think. And I've heard that the men who are closest to him spurn the women. But Joshua himself helps women as much as he helps men. He'll help me if I can only get to him." Her voice grew stronger. "I will get to him. I will find someone of strong arms and a willing heart."

I stood with legs that would collapse if they had their own way. I forced them to be solid. My whole life had prepared me to make this journey, carrying this child. My whole life. I lifted the sleeping girl child from the pagan woman's arms with care and gratitude.

CHAPTER THIRTEEN

Lucia walked with more stamina than I had expected. Her need to save her daughter strengthened her legs and lungs. When I would ask her if she wanted a rest, she'd shake her head in silence. I admired her determination, for a rest would have sorely tested the patience of my soul.

We followed the riverbed again, this time going north, of course. The great river connected the Dead Sea to the Sea of Galilee. It was the shortest, truest path. I had traveled much of this route only little more than a half year before, but in the opposite direction. I looked at everything, expecting to recognize landmarks here and there. Instead, the world stood new and fresh before me. I went as swiftly as my companions could bear, for there was no reason to delay now. The final words of the final canticle infused my spirit:

Make haste, my beloved, and be thou like to a roe or to a young hart upon the mountains of spices.

The child Martina remained patient in my arms, though I knew the trip was tedious at best and painful at worst. She didn't complain and groans escaped her rarely. Lucia sang to her almost constantly, even when the child slept. I knew she sang to comfort herself. I recognized the habit.

We rested finally and Lucia bathed Martina at the river's edge. Then she produced from within her cloak small, hardened, sweet rolls rich with raisins. I washed my hands and offered the Creator my thanks and ate, while Martina nestled in her mother's lap. The child's eyes were wide and curious now. Despite the heat in her cheeks, she looked around, restless. Yet I knew she'd have no ability to run and play. My heart went out to a child that needed to play but could only watch.

I opened my cloth bag and took out the flute which had lain dormant too long. I played the tune that Lucia had sung.

Martina smiled the purity of childhood. I would have done anything to keep that smile on her face.

Lucia sang now, and my flute sent out strings that wove a pattern through her mysterious Latin words. When she stopped, I went to put the flute away in the bag, for my hands needed to be free to carry the child.

"May I, Miriam?" Lucia put out her hand. "I play a little myself."

I gave Lucia the flute and she yielded Martina into my arms. We got up and walked. Lucia put her lips to the flute and played. And how she played. She was more expert than even Judith. The melodies she knew were strange and lovely to my ear.

"Did you like that?" Lucia's voice betrayed her eagerness to hear my response.

I was surprised and oddly excited. What did it matter to Lucia whether or not her music

touched my heart when her whole day was fo-
cused on the ailing state of Martina? Yet it did.

And I was glad that it did. I, too, wanted to give
pleasure with my music. I answered honestly,
anxious to see her reaction. "My feet would have
danced gleefully to that music when I was
younger."

Lucia let out her breath in relief. "That's
good."

"Lucia, tell me . . ." I stopped.

She put her hand on mine. "What, Maria?"

Her sudden Romanization of my name was
unexpected, yet not unpleasant. "You are
plagued with troubles. I am no stranger to misery." I swallowed the hot desert air. "And still
we sing."

Lucia blew gently on Martina's forehead and
tucked the child's curls behind her ears. "My
people have a saying. 'Without its stones, a
stream would lose its song.'"

And yes. Finally things were making sense. I
wished I could tell Abraham. I was happy, so
very happy. I found my mouth opening and I was
singing, from the *Song of Songs*, of course,

singing songs of passionate love to the fragile child in my arms.

> *Behold, thou art fair, my love;*
> *behold, thou art fair;*
> *thou hast dove's eyes within thy locks:*
> *thy hair is as a flock of goats,*
> *that appear from Mount Gilead.*
> *Thy teeth are like a flock of sheep*
> *that are even shorn,*
> *which came up from the washing;*
> *whereof every one bears twins, and none is*
> *barren among them.*
> *Thy lips are like a thread of scarlet*
> *and thy speech is comely . . .*

I sang and held Martina close. Her slender fingers moved to my voice.

Lucia spoke Hebrew well, this I knew by now. She marveled at the words of the canticles. She listened closely and by nightfall, she was humming along. By midway through the second day, she was singing, as well.

Before long we joined other travelers heading north. At first I thought they must be seeking baptism at Jochanan's hands. But when we rested, I learned of Jochanan's fate. The man who had called for all to return to a gentler age had been killed. His head had been served on a platter to Salome, the stepdaughter of Herod Antipas. I wanted to scream for that silent head. I wanted to bleed on Salome's hands and leave an uncleanliness that could never be washed away, a mark that would tell the world forever who she truly was. Herod Antipas had worried that Jochanan the Baptist would incite the people to insurrection. The Romans feared revolt from every corner. Poor innocent, angry Jochanan. Though I myself was not drawn to follow Jochanan, though I myself had no desire to follow any man, I knew that Jochanan had traveled a personal road, not a political one. Poor raving Baptist. The man whose only true goal was a revolution of the soul had been slaughtered like an animal by another animal. Jochanan had become *terefah*, unclean flesh. No one would be nourished by his death. Senseless slaughter.

I learned from my fellow travelers that before Jochanan was arrested and thrown in the prison at Machaerus near the Dead Sea so close to where I had been living all these months, he baptized the great healer and they worked side by side at the river. These travelers here headed now for Galilee, just like Lucia and Martina and me. *Joshua* was on everyone's lips.

My mind raced through these facts. If the Romans had arrested Jochanan, Jochanan who didn't cure anyone, who no one called king, then surely they would soon arrest the man called Joshua. We had to place Martina in Joshua's hands while he still lived.

I walked faster, as fast as I could without wearing out Lucia. We passed every group of travelers we met. Our songs sped our steps. And each step increased my urgency. I had to hear this Joshua talk. I had to know him. And if he was truly a healer, then, oh yes, I would help him. I looked down at Martina, who slept now in my arms, and I knew that I had finally found my calling. If Joshua was who people claimed he was, he needed me.

As we drew closer to Galilee, we learned that Joshua was in the town of Capernaum. Capernaum was an easy hour's walk beyond Magdala. We would pass directly by my home town.

The thought came to me slowly, putting itself forward as a vague desire at first, then finally rising from its shyness to take clean shape: I would stop in Magdala. If I saw no one familiar, I would go to my home and kiss Father and Judith and Hannah one last time. If I saw people I feared would recognize me, I'd turn away quickly and go only to the graves under the terebinth and the sycamore. Whatever happened, I would visit those three graves.

I led Lucia to the outskirts of town and handed her Martina. "I have an errand. Go now to the house of prayer in Magdala. Anyone you meet can point out the way. You can rest there. If I can, I will meet you at sunset here on the road. But if I'm not back by sunset, you have nothing to fear. You can walk to Capernaum by yourself. You can carry Martina there, I promise you. The road is short and level."

Lucia wanted to protest. I could see the fear in her eyes. She was tired and weak. Yet she kept herself from asking me to stay with her. Perhaps she responded to the need in my eyes. Judith used to be able to read my eyes — maybe Lucia had the same gift. I wished I could take her as far as the house of prayer, but I didn't want her with me if I was recognized. I wouldn't expose her and Martina to that.

I took the flute from my bag, the flute we had shared on this journey. "When Martina is well again, teach her." I slipped the flute into Lucia's bag. Then I kissed her, I kissed my Roman friend, my singing companion. I kissed her daughter.

I stayed on the main road, but within fifteen minutes I realized I had to take to the alleys. There were crowds in Magdala today. I'd never seen such crowds. Surely among all those people someone would recognize me, even behind my veil, even in my now tattered dress. I skirted along the alleys, in and out, my heart pressing against my ribs. I passed the little street where Jacob kept his carpenter's shop. Dread squeezed my throat and for a moment I lost my breath. Grief and rage fought within me. If I stood at that corner long enough, perhaps he would pass. Perhaps I could look upon his face — maybe even into his eyes. And what did I hope to see there? Jacob's mind was no better than wood.

I kept on moving. I came up to our house from the rear. I went around the outside, looking carefully every which way for following eyes. Then I knocked on the door. When no one answered, I went in.

The house was empty. I walked from object to object, running my hands over the familiar woods and clays. I buried my face in Judith's pillow and breathed deep of her sweet odors. I kissed the handles on the water jar that Hannah's fingers gripped every day. I spilled tears on the tassels of Father's tallith, folded neatly on the shelf. Me, the one who went dry-eyed for two years, who had finally cried in the wilderness on the way to see Jochanan the Baptist, I was now a virtual fountain of tears. But these were tears of joy. Father and Judith and Hannah were well. This home spoke of their health and wholeness. Had they gotten the message I sent via Uncle? Did they think I was traveling with my husband? Did they envision me in Jerusalem, eating heartily, perhaps heavy with child? I would leave them with that vision.

I went out the door quickly and ran. I sat on the earth halfway between the terebinth and the sycamore. I sang. Not the canticles this time. I sang songs I had made up in my months in the caves. Songs of morning and noon and night. Songs of juniper trees and mimosa and dates. Songs of the hawk and the sparrow, of the ox and the camel. Songs of women working together. Songs of men and women loving one another. Songs of mother and child. I breathed in the penetrating scent of the terebinth, until it perfumed my very soul. I picked a ripe sycamore fig and ate it reverently, remembering the kindness of the whore the night Isaac died.

Abraham's cart was full of dry sycamore leaves, three autumns' worth. I dug a small hole in the center of the leaves. Then I took the stone from my belt — that stone that had been the color of pomegranate when I first found it, but was all milk and moonlight now. I remembered patting the pomegranate juice from Abraham's chin when we were children. I remembered the stain on my fingers, on his fingers. I buried my polished stone in the cart. I needed no solid token of the loves behind me. My past was with me, in me. My past would carry me forward.

I walked back toward Lucia. I hurried, for there was nothing to keep me here any longer. And there was no time to lose in finding Joshua. I thought I'd circle around the well and then take the alleys. That would be shortest, quickest. But when I came out upon the well, I realized my mistake. There were many women at the well. They talked heatedly. I learned why there were so many crowds in the streets of Magdala that day: Joshua had come to town. Joshua was here in Magdala at this very moment. He was outside the house of prayer. Perhaps his hand was already cooling the fever in Martina's forehead. Oh, yes. It was. I knew it was! I felt the flush race to my cheeks.

I turned to go back into the bushes and make a wider arc around them. But I turned too late.

"Who is that?"

"It's Miriam! Look!"

"Why has she returned?"

"Yes, why?"

"She slept with the idiot!"

"I heard that, too."

"The whore!"

Something hit me in the shoulder hard and I stumbled to my knees. That one pause was enough to give them time to surround me.

"Get away from here."

"You bring only trouble!"

"I'm looking for the healer," I said. I stood up.

"The healer? What illness do you have?"

"Why are you at our well? Do you spill your poisoned spirit in our waters?"

More women came. Their eyes held righteous indignation.

I ran then. I ran through their circle and straight down the road toward the town center, toward the house of prayer. I heard shouts behind me. Shouts of men now. I felt the fury of a people confused, a people prepared to fend off evil.

The crowd threatened to turn into a mob in an instant. I was fast and strong, but I was also tired from my long journey. My dress held me back. I tried to get away. I did my best.

The hand that grabbed me by the shoulder dug in. I spun around to face a blow in the stomach. Someone ripped at my hair from behind. Hands shredded my clothes from all sides. And the fit came. The seventh fit. My final fit. Oh, blessed fit, that marked the passage from one way of life to another. The whole world shimmered in divine light.

A woman's voice screamed out above the crowd. "Stand back for Joshua. Stand back!"

And then a man said, "Let her be."

I felt their hands no longer. I heard nothing more. I saw nothing I could recognize. I was beyond this world.

Then it was over. Just like every other time. Gone. My chest heaved with coughs. Then silence. I lay on the dirt road and looked at the sky. The blue, blue sky.

I turned my head. In the crowd I saw Martina standing beside Lucia. The girl on her feet, looking steadily at me. I felt the joy of my future even then. I stood slowly.

A hand took mine. The man attached to this hand was small and thin and ugly, an unlikely man for the mission the Creator had given him. His eyes contrasted boldly with his rich, dark skin, for they were the color of the Sea of Galilee. The color of the heavens. His hand was strong — a hand with useful fingers like my own — a hand with purpose. He was the Jew I had come to help, the healer who needed my help. "Welcome, Magdalene." Joshua turned to the crowds and announced the wisdom that Abraham had tried his best to teach me so long ago: "This woman has no devils within her. Not seven, not one. None."

I traveled with Joshua, the healer that the Romans called Jesus, all the way to Jerusalem. Just as I had told Uncle and Rachel I would do. We gathered beggars everywhere. And we gathered the infirm. And I kept an alabaster jar of ointments always ready, for there were many bodies to comfort. And I kept a song in my mouth always ready, for there were many souls to heal.

EPILOGUE

Mary Magdalene first appears in the New Testament with Jesus, either anointing his feet or coming forth among the afflicted, asking to be healed. Biblical scholars disagree over this. But the one thing scholars agree on is that the New Testament tells us nothing of the life of Mary prior to meeting Jesus. I worked backward, starting with every biblical episode I could find that might possibly involve Mary Magdalene (a challenging task, since there are several Marys in the early New Testament), and then creating for her a history that would prepare her for and help make sense of the actions she takes in the New Testament.

The excerpts from the *Song of Songs* are adapted from the King James Version of *The Holy Bible* with minor modifications.